C000153963

Being in her early twenties and living in limbo, Harriet Mills set out to do something she swore throughout her creative writing degree that she would never do—write a novel.

It may sound strange considering her degree choice, yet fiction was never her chosen form, instead she thought a career in journalism would be the path that she would take after studies.

This was until she discovered more about life, about people and about stories. Working in a local village store in the place she grew up, Harriet's mind acted like a sponge when she discovered that an interesting read would be one about life itself.

The uniqueness of the place she worked in gave her the ideas, her visit to Dublin gave her the setting and a fond love of words gave her the ability to get it all down into her debut novel—*Dear Brannagh*.

30·11·20

Inspired by Granddad's memoirs and Granny's photo, both writers at heart.

Harriet Mills

DEAR BRANNAGH

AUSTIN MACAULEY PUBLISHERS™

LONDON · CAMBRIDGE · NEW YORK · SHARJAH

Copyright © Harriet Mills (2020)

The right of Harriet Mills to be identified as author of this work has been asserted by the author in accordance with section 77 and 78 of the Copyright, Designs and Patents Act 1988.

All rights reserved. No part of this publication may be reproduced, stored in a retrieval system, or transmitted in any form or by any means, electronic, mechanical, photocopying, recording, or otherwise, without the prior permission of the publishers.

Any person who commits any unauthorised act in relation to this publication may be liable to criminal prosecution and civil claims for damages.

This is a work of fiction. Names, characters, businesses, places, events, locales, and incidents are either the products of the author's imagination or used in a fictitious manner. Any resemblance to actual persons, living or dead, or actual events is purely coincidental.

A CIP catalogue record for this title is available from the British Library.

ISBN 9781528997447 (Paperback)
ISBN 9781528997454 (ePub e-book)

www.austinmacauley.com

First Published (2020)
Austin Macauley Publishers Ltd
25 Canada Square
Canary Wharf
London
E14 5LQ

I would like to thank my huge support network that I have surrounding me.

I would like to thank, my parents, for urging me to believe that it is good to be different, to take risks and to follow your dream; my bosses, Kathy and Mike, for being so much more than your average bosses and encouraging me with pride to never "86 it"; all my tutors at York St John University and the brilliant English teachers I have had for giving me the confidence to put my writing out there; my friends and the many customers and connections that I got through my job at the stores for proofreading, editing and for giving advice before I got any further; Teresa and Julia, for sharing their experiences; Austin Macauley Publishers, for giving me this huge opportunity.

I would like to thank everyone who believed in me.

Prologue

Saturday, 13 August 1988

Dear Brannagh,

Phew, I feel exhausted. Travelling and all has taken it out of me but also the whole emotional turmoil of everything and not knowing what to expect. I'm only little!

Dinner went well, and I kept to the etiquette okay. Sandra is extremely stylish and elegant in her ways; it's intimidating! Though, I am sure she's nice.

They showed us around their house which is the biggest I think I have ever seen, at least that I have ever been inside. The whole street is full of huge properties behind grand gates that open on command as if the car does it for them.

Oh yeah, that brings me to the ride from the airport to here. We were in a black taxi, you know like the ones you find on TV. It was very cool to be inside one.

We sat around the table, and all was well. Dinner was delicious, and I can tell that for however long we stay here we are going to be treated right. The only thing was that I sensed some tension between Derek and Daddy.

It was so obvious. I don't even know who Derek is, and Daddy has certainly never mentioned him to me, but there was something not right about their relationship. It might just be because they haven't seen each other for a while, so it's a little awkward to think of things to say, but I'd have thought that would make it less awkward because you have so much to say!

Anyway, as I say, I'm only little! How's Ireland?

All my love, Mary xx

Sunday, 4 September 1988

Dear Brannagh,

My new house is great. Derek and Sandra are the loveliest couple, and they are treating Daddy and me like we're royalty of some sort. I like England as well. Well, what I have seen so far anyway. We went to see Buckingham Palace the other day, and it was amazing. Beyond my expectations and just so huge. The crowds were also massive, so we didn't stay too long; you know what old people are like with crowds. To be honest, I didn't like the amount of people around either, so I didn't mind.

That's the thing really. My time in England so far has been in a bubble, and I haven't had to make new friends or try too hard in social situations. The only people I have been socialising with have been Derek and Sandra, who are making all the effort and Daddy who I don't need to try with.

I'm so scared, Brannagh, I start school tomorrow. It's like being thrown in the deep end to a pool of Sharks. I can't remember how to start talking to people. Hopefully, they will be nice, Sandra convinces me that they will.

How is Ireland anyway?

All my love, Mary

Xx

Thursday, 17 March 1994

Dear Brannagh,

Firstly, HAPPY ST PADDY'S DAY! I hope you're celebrating like they taught us how to.

Secondly, I haven't written to you in a while, so thought it was about time. Also, I am in a MASSIVE dilemma, so, I need your help.

You know my luck with guys hasn't been great… up until now. I met this guy at uni. He's totally good looking and way above my league, but I don't care because last month we went on the most perfect date together, and I had sex with him. Oh my gosh, it was amazing, and I feel so confident now.

Anyway, losing my virginity is another matter altogether, more importantly, now I am completely confused because I haven't heard from him since. I'm panicking about all the usual kind of shite like, *was I awful in bed or did I say the most horrendously cringe-worthy thing and it put him off for life*. I'm even scared that he is a typical English boy and being all polite, that he didn't enjoy the date at all but didn't want to say.

I know you'll have some words to put my mind at ease.

Hope you're doing grand and all that. I best get ready for our Paddy's day celebrations now.

All my love, Mary
Xx

Sunday, 1 April 2018

Dear Mary,

I'm so sorry that I've not been in touch for such a long time. You know how life is. I struggle to spend enough time with Mammy, and I live right near her, but I guess that's part of growing up, right?

Just got back from McD's. Still such a good crack, but I had to leave. Darn it. Had a few Guinness for you. I know how much you like a pint of the black stuff in Dublin. You need to come back. Like you REALLY need to come back.

Mary, what I'm really trying to tell you is that I need you. I don't mean I need you to write to me with lovely words like you always do, but I NEED you. I need to meet you, and I need your help. I'm in some trouble. It's Daniel, and I don't know what to do. Mary, I'm scared. He hurts me. Badly. And it's suddenly got so much worse.

Brannagh xx

Chapter 1
Dublin, 2018

I had forgotten how magical this place had once made me feel until now, experiencing the magic all over again. I didn't think for one minute that this would be the case, but I suddenly feel in control and at home. It's almost as if I've forgotten my motive for the trip altogether, and for a moment, which feels longer than I imagine it is, I am enjoying this pleasant sensation and am at peace.

I have returned at a crucial time which becomes clearer to me as I see the abortion campaigns plastering the streets. I would have thought thirty years ago that this would have passed by 2018 and that the women of Ireland would have the freedom to choose. Instead, the 'No' campaigners are not giving up their fight, attacking women across Ireland to feel guilty for having a choice.

'At 22 weeks I have fingernails, don't repel me,' reads one sign from the angry campaigners, desperately clinging onto the past and not accepting the different circumstances that women find themselves in. 'A woman you love might need your yes,' reads a board from the opposing side. I'm with the latter, giving women a choice and stopping hundreds who flee to England to safely abort a child that may not survive or abandon the memory of horrific and unwanted intercourse. There are individual stories, and this needs to be addressed, but then that is only my opinion after all.

I ponder the debate for a while in blissful silence which is a miracle considering the company I am in. Erin has just bought new headphones, so whilst ignoring the hardworking driver's commentary, she's listening to her Spotify playlist entitled 'Musicals' while Jack innocently attempts to grasp every word that the cheerful and witty commentator utters, adult jokes going straight over his head which I am thankful for.

I can't believe how much this place has changed and how much my life has changed since I was here. Mammy instantly returns to my memory, and though she doesn't cross it much these days, it is comforting to feel. I don't really know why I have returned anymore. At least, in this current moment I haven't a clue.

A tear drops from the corner of my eye which, together with the rare Dublin sunshine, forces me to put my sunglasses on. It's a tear of happiness, of sheer contentment which I haven't felt much at all for as long as I can remember. This place represents the start of everything for me, and though I'm not as good as Jack, and I'm ignoring every word that the driver is saying due to my mind wandering elsewhere, I think to myself how different things could have been.

'Stop number twenty-two,' the driver calls out. 'The Guinness Storehouse.' I've never been, and right now I could demolish a pint of the black stuff like Daddy would if he were here with us, but with two young children, I think I'll pass. Most couples leave the top deck and prepare to stand in the long queue having missed the memo about pre-booking to avoid it. I look up to the top and dream about sitting alone in the Gravity bar staring out mindlessly onto the Wicklow Mountains in the distance. Then I'm suddenly back in reality when Jack claims he's desperate for a wee. I guess we'll be getting off at stop number twenty-three then.

As the bus pulls off and has a near miss with the numerous horse and carriages which scatter the streets, I smile again at my uplifted spirit. Each carriage has a couple of jolly Irishmen on board, controlling the erratic, hot and tired horses, though probably just as happy as everybody else is for some rare sunshine in the city.

I quickly scan the map to find that stop number twenty-three is the Irish Museum of Modern Art, which though I'm sure they've spent a lot of time catering for youngsters wouldn't be the right place for mine. Jack wouldn't be too difficult though he'd never join in, or speak come to that, yet Erin wouldn't even contemplate giving it her time. She's at that age, the dreaded teenage years.

Jack's need to urinate strengthens as does the whining in my ear every five seconds, so I look forward to stop number twenty-four—Heuston Station. Somewhere nearby is bound to have public toilets or a tree that he can hide behind.

While holding the large green plan in both hands, I am suddenly struck with the alienation I feel from this place nowadays, having to look at a map to get my bearings. I used to know it off by heart. Mostly, the four walls of McDinton's, but I knew it nonetheless. I appreciate that below the age of fourteen seems a little early to be spending your days in a pub, but when your daddy owns it, you're in Ireland, and the majority of custom comes from the drunkards within your own family, it's then deemed okay I suppose.

Erin rolls her eyes as I neatly fold the map away and put it back in my handbag knowing how embarrassing I'll look in her view. I've refused to allow her to get an iPhone up until now and will remain stubborn only allowing music devices for fear she'll get hooked and become just another youth glued to their screen. However, I am aware that she knows all about them and how much cooler I would look if I learnt how to control the voice on the Google Maps application to guide me around instead of the humiliatingly ancient method—the paper version.

The traffic is rapidly increasing in anticipation of the Ed Sheeran concert at Phoenix Park tonight, so I have already decided that we will walk to that because I can't cope with the moans that would come from my children while waiting in an hour-long jam. Jack is already arguing about why he has to go, but he will love it once there, I hope.

We finally reach the chosen stop, and I mouth to Erin that it's time to get off which she huffs at, somehow knowing the reason that we're departing despite having been zoned out with *Les Misérables* blasting into her eardrum for the past half an hour. It comforts me that she still enjoys the music from her favourite West End shows. Recently, she's hit the phase that every girl reaches when they get to the age of thirteen, so I'm told, and it worries me that she will totally lose her childhood charm. In fact, the only time that she shows any ounce of childlike excitement these days, or a genuine smile come to that, is when we board the train from York to London Kings Cross to see a show.

Luckily, we find a small café along the street and pop in for a much-needed caffeine fix and toilet stop for Jack. Whilst they are enjoying a delicious slice of cake and hot chocolates, I get a smile out of both of my children and feel warm inside as if for once I am doing a good job.

I stopped working at St Peter's at the end of the Autumn-term five years ago and haven't been back since due to everything that has happened, but I feel more exhausted now than I ever felt at work. I'm starting to think that work was my break because being a mother comes with so many worries and stresses that childless teachers just couldn't understand. I love it, of course I do, and cherish moments like this with my children, but it doesn't remove the ability that they have to force blood pressure levels to rise to unhealthy readings.

After enough rest and the right amount of hot chocolate spillages on Jack's part to remove the worry that he too is growing up too fast, I wait for Erin to go to the toilet so that I can reveal the trusty map in public and not cause her face to go bright red with embarrassment. I work out where the next stop is in relation to the café, and we head to catch the bus to the zoo.

It's times like these when I miss an adult companion. I thoroughly enjoy spending quality time with the children and think that it's so important to keep doing so until they stubbornly refuse to partake in my plans. Even at that point, I will put up a good fight to keep them under my wing. Nevertheless, there are always moments when I'm alone with them where I seek adult conversation. Or even somebody who truly knows to tell me that I'm doing everything right or that it will all be okay in the end. I've always found that saying peculiar. When exactly is the end? I'd rather know before I reach my deathbed that things have got better and the past has remained where it belongs.

Jack's innocent face lights up when he spots the green bus approaching our stop, and I rush into my busy handbag to find where I've put the tickets. Erin smugly stands with her hand held out.

'Oh Mother, you gave them to me to look after. At least, one of us is on the ball today.' I sigh with a slight smile and take them from her.

'Thank you, darling.'

She will have a strong control of her life in the future, I always think. She will hold it all together no matter what life throws at her. She has done extremely well so far, they both have, and they have even kept me going at times, so I know that Erin is going to take life firmly in her stride.

We head straight to the top deck and enjoy more of the summer breeze and commentary. I focus on a mixture of sounds but primarily hear 'The Dubliners' singing in between the knowledgeable and witty driver talking about the development of Guinness. He tells us how it was effectively made by mistake when the brewers burnt the hop and sold it off cheaply to people who loved the taste, so it stuck. Good work, I say. Hearing all this history, which, of course, is largely evolved around drinking makes me feel very grounded and at home.

To my surprise Erin hasn't had her headphones in for this segment of our trip and has been happily listening to the insightful information about Dublin. Perhaps she's destined to follow in my footsteps and will too develop a drinking problem later in life, I think to myself, quite negatively. Perhaps keeping her entertained throughout our time at the zoo won't be such a headache after all, I consider more optimistically.

Forty-four Euros and forty cents to get us three in the gate which hugely reiterates how glad I am that Erin and Jack have outgrown the novelty of gift shops already. Nothing is cheap these days, but it's all part of the fun. I may allow them to have an ice cream at the end as an incentive to pretend to enjoy themselves, which is a stimulant mostly directed towards Erin. Then we'll find somewhere nice to eat. Another extortionate blowout that the half-term holidays bring, but something else that has to be done.

It's been a while since I've visited a zoo, and prior to having children, it was an activity that never appealed to me. Spending most of my childhood in the pub and watching drunken relatives make total fools of themselves but in complete merriment, the zoo was never an option. However, Mammy did take me a couple of times when there was nothing else that she could think of for school holiday entertainment. She'd often palm me off to a friend or Aunt Eileen so that she could remain in control of everything else in her life without the distraction of a young, excitable child. What an inconvenience I sometimes was!

My mind wanders again while walking among the animals, and I deliberate over how much cheaper it would have been to park up on a grassy spot in Phoenix Park with a picnic and let my mind go there. Erin would cope, but Jack needs the stimulation of doing and seeing things to keep him occupied, so I'm not regretting this expense too much for the sake of my sanity.

After an hour and a half, meandering through the cages and too much time spent laughing at the monkey's, even Jack has had enough. They both refuse my generous offer of ice cream and want to head straight out for some food. I almost gasp when I notice the time is three o'clock already and swiftly take their first answer as final as we head towards the city centre, but not too far in so that the menus supposedly remain cheaper.

Although I still struggle to understand every word that Jack says, I sense the excitement he has about the zoo and all he has to say about it. As we walk and Erin lags behind probably choosing which song to overplay next, he doesn't stop chattering away, so I let the words flow, making out a few of the clearer sentences to which I can reply. It's another lovely moment just chatting to my boy, and the need for adult companionship in this instant vanishes.

The kids are after pizza, so each Pizzeria we pass, I stop to compare prices. Acknowledging their lack of food connoisseur skills, I know that I'll just pick the cheapest one, the great mother that I am. We settle on a lovely, but still pricy, restaurant just off the main street facing the river and Temple Bar. Luckily, we've beaten the rush so getting a table is not difficult, and my children both opt for Margherita highlighting their plain appetites (though I'm secretly grinning at their decisions seeing the price of the other options). I'm not stingy with money, and we've never been short, but I like to be careful. Besides, as soon as children enter the equation life triples in value regardless.

The gates to Ed Sheeran open at five, so I'm constantly aware of the time while we're eating, removing dessert as an option, and instead I buy them sweets from a newsagent that we pass on the way as a means of energy for the long walk to Phoenix Park. I know that once we reach it, it's only going to be the beginning of our journey, but I keep that knowledge to myself to avoid the dramatic moans that would come from my children if I made them aware. As we fight the crowds which increase significantly every hundred metres, I consider tying a child to each wrist, but then figure I'm being a little over the top. I do squeeze Jack tight to my side though and ensure one eye is on Erin at all times.

Amazed by the busyness and the excitement of seeing police everywhere, neither Jack nor Erin are saying much which allows me headspace to consider this place that was once my home, the memories it holds and all that has happened since. This is too much for my brain to cope with, but I have no control of it going AWOL each time it gets a chance.

I think back to my days with Dr Knoll and the mindfulness exercises she gave me. The typical five four three two one, the one that I found the easiest to remember. At times of despair or when my mind was beginning to go a little crazy, I was to think of five things I can see, four things I can hear, three things I can smell, two things I can feel and one thing I can taste. That might not be the order, but it always seemed to help me.

I try to take in my surroundings to focus my mind on something other than horror and take in all the lovely town houses which appear every now and then on the side streets from the main road leading to Phoenix Park. I choose my favourites and which I could see myself living in most. This is something that is never going to be an option because I'm very happy in York, but it's still fun to fantasise anyway.

One particular set of steps draws me in. Everything around me stops, and the busyness vanishes as if I'm a protagonist in a film. Everything gets slower, and I take in the face of the individual sat on the third step down. I've never seen a face so expressionless as the one before me. They could have just discovered that they have been granted a dream position in the firm that they never thought they could be part of, or they could have been told that their father has just died. As the face lifts out of the palms of the two hands that hold it, I am forced to stop in my stride, fully aware of how late we already are for beating the crowds to the concert.

It is a face I know but have never met. One that brings with it extreme warmth but all of the horror, guilt and sadness mixed in. It instantly churns up my past for me to face it all over again. It is a face that has been with me from the age of thirteen yet somehow is younger by five years or more. A face I never thought I would meet but is about to look me directly in the eye.

Chapter 2
February 1994

It was a Saturday morning, so Mary's body clock had drilled into her the pleasure of a day off, forgetting entirely that she'd agreed to meet Charlotte in the library before her exciting date. She was known for it, but this time even she surprised herself with her lateness and quickly leapt out of bed to begin what seemed in that instant a mission impossible.

First year hadn't been thrilling so far for Mary, and despite doing well in all her exams, she felt it was missing something more. She had heard so many stories about the university experience and how most women met their husbands there, but so far her male companionship hadn't reached further than a library buddy or someone to sit beside in a lecture hall. Neither of whom she could see herself copulating with on anything other than a desperate level.

That was why James Carter asking her out on a date was something which she already found very special. She didn't particularly know him besides from the obvious which every girl who had ever set foot inside the grounds of the university knew. These factors included his gorgeous looks, Rugby expertise being captain of the Men's first team and her surprise at him acknowledging her because he was one of the coolest guys on campus.

First, she had to meet Charlotte though so that she could keep up the good grades and make her father proud as well as obtaining a high-level degree for her future. She had a sensible mindset like that, most of the time. Charlotte had found some useful material in the library for their research project which saved Mary a load of work. It was always good to maintain friendships like that, Mary thought, as she grabbed whichever garment showed the most cleavage from her wardrobe while constantly fighting the ticking clock. Useful friendships meant that Mary didn't have to waste time searching when she could be spending her time hunting down the man that her life was missing.

Most of her friends were in relationships, and if they weren't then they were in the category of the few friends she had who stuck their noses in books. This wasn't on an interestingly artsy level developing a range of recommendations and fascinating conversation, but rather one that was more nerdy and dull. These were the ones that she had been friends with since she moved to England and would rather let go of so she could liven her life up a little as harsh as it sounded.

It was a good job that her university library was only a five-minute walk away because she would have a lot more late marks next to her name if it wasn't. She had a habit of never leaving enough time to get sorted no matter how hard she tried and, in this instance, she had left Charlotte a half hour slot before she was due to meet James, so time was tight before she had even started getting ready. It would have worked out perfectly if she wasn't still in her pyjama bottoms with her hair a mess from the food fight that she had had with her housemates the night before. She rushed to get ready in record speed when Jas walked in still semi-intoxicated with a shirt on that belonged to last night's lover.

'Last night was hilarious, did you see him?' she asked, laughing and slurring her words. 'I'm not sure if he's left yet, but nobody is in my bed anymore, and if he's hiding somewhere, I'm ready for more.'

'Jas, I love your stories, I really do. Each day they make me smile, and one day we'll turn it all into a book, but for now I'm incredibly late and may get laid myself later, so would really appreciate some peace.'

Jas left the room making a face to Mary that only two sisters would make to each other in a silly, childish argument and headed downstairs for something to soak up the alcohol.

The girls had a great setup within the house, knowing each other's personalities exactly, so no offence was ever taken. They knew all about Mary's ways, blunt and to the point like her dad. In fact, when he first visited, Mary had to warn them all of this. He was Mary multiplied by one hundred, and he would have made some of them cry if they hadn't been pre-warned about his and Mary's humour because they were always just having a joke.

By some miracle, Mary made it to the library in time with twenty minutes to dedicate to listening to Charlotte explain her notes, when really she could just have handed them over. Mary went with it knowing what Charlotte was like and left for the Minster which was where she was due to meet James at 1 pm.

Charlotte could have stayed chatting for hours at the library, but Mary had to use her father's ways and cut her off sharply so that her date wasn't left waiting. It was lucky she left when she did because the bus was just pulling up to the stop when she strolled up to it. A sign that it was going to be a good day, she hoped.

She caught the newly established bus service which linked the university campus with the city centre, half smiling, half nervous wreck throughout the journey. A girl sat to her left put her at ease as she was chatting to a friend about an interview she was attending that day but didn't think she'd get it having received awful news of her father's passing late the night before. Things could definitely be worse, Mary thought, and she knew how the girl would have felt to some extent, so her heart sank a little empathetically for the stranger.

As she headed through the middle of town towards the glorious Minster, she felt like a sixteen-year-old preparing for her first kiss. She was all gooey inside which was strange because aside from a few exchanged notes when passing each other in uni and a phone call to sort this meet, she hadn't had anything to do with James except to admire him from afar.

As soon as she saw him stood glaring up at the huge building in front of him, smiling to himself when he turned around and saw her walking up to him, she admired him more than ever. He was the perfect height for Mary and his looks accentuated her nerves. She immediately felt as though she was punching above her weight. Though she knew deep down that no matter who she first dated, her lack of self-confidence would have made her feel that way. She was running through everything in her head at rapid speed which made it worse because she couldn't think of what to say when she got close enough to address him. It was as if she'd forgotten all knowledge of communication altogether and couldn't even think up a simple 'hello'. Luckily, he appeared more relaxed and took control to open the conversation.

'Well, aren't you looking lovely? Thank you for meeting me, I was beginning to think you'd stood me up.'

James spoke with complete confidence, and all sentences that left his mouth came out smoothly as if someone had written him a script which he had rehearsed over and over until he had perfected his lines. Mary's awkward giggle left him leeway for another line of the script because her brain had still misplaced the English language.

'I was thinking of grabbing some lunch and a cheeky beer or two, how does that sound?'

The question, directed at Mary, allowed her brain to sort itself out so that she could prove to James that speech wasn't something that she lacked, and talking was another one of her talents.

'That'd be great,' she said with a sheepish smile.

He took her arm and guided it through the bend in his, and they walked along the cobbled streets of York. It was at this point when Mary felt thankful that she had opted for flat shoes instead of trying to impress him with heels because that would have made room for a whole other level of embarrassment when she inevitably stacked it straight away.

It was a cool but bright day, and York was looking even more stunning in the sunshine. Town was heaving with people, and with the streets being rather narrow, they felt it was best to find a pub sooner rather than waiting for their frustration to build behind slow walkers, ruining the happiness which was felt between the two of them from the start.

Thankfully, Goodramgate wasn't far away, home to one of James' favourite haunts.

They only had to dodge the enthusiastic fudge seller outside the little red shop on Low Petergate and pass through the crowds watching the busker at Café Rouge. He was always there, and whoever allowed him permission to setup in such an awkward area of a narrow street needed sacking from their job, Mary always thought. However, the warm sweet smell of freshly made fudge that lingered along the road soon shifted Mary's thoughts to a more positive place.

The Old White Swann was a typical English pub full of warmth and oldness. As they entered on this cold February afternoon, it hadn't reached its peak like most of the other pubs in York on a Saturday and was comfortably busy but with seats available by the roaring fire. Spotting this, they decided to grab a drink and sit a while before heading into the restaurant for some food. James was doing a great job of taking control like a true gentleman and asked Mary what she would like to drink while pointing to the seats that he wanted her to occupy while waiting for him to bring her said beverage.

Mary was comfortable with this, and James' attitude, which so far implied that he treated women well, made her fancy him even more. She wouldn't describe herself as overly shy, but in social situations like this one she felt the pressure, and her slight lack of self-esteem exaggerated this feeling. Though she knew as they got to know each other more and consumed a few more beverages to loosen up a little, then all would be okay, and she'd forget all about her nerves.

She had opted for a pint of lager; Carlsberg was what they had on tap. She forgot feminine etiquette whenever she entered a pub and proved an element of truth to the Irish stereotype, only drinking pints and never doing things by halves. James had gone for the same, and his grin remained as he headed over with both drinks in hand, sipping at his so that it didn't spill but spilling a little of hers as he went.

'I'll be measuring which has the most in it before I choose so I'm not short-changed you know,' Mary declared in jest.

It was the first sentence she had uttered with confidence, and she was proud of herself for doing so. Instantly, the atmosphere went from happy but a little tense to totally relaxed, and they hadn't even consumed alcohol yet.

The two sat chatting by the fire for a couple of drinks and then headed to the restaurant to line their stomachs for whatever the day held. Mary was feeling a little tipsy already because in the rush of her morning, she had forgotten to eat anything, so she was very glad that James had decided to eat in the restaurant, so she would get a substantial meal inside her and not make a fool of herself too soon.

As the minutes passed, she felt more and more comfortable in his company, and it was as if James never questioned his comfort in hers. She felt like she had known him longer than just a few hours and hadn't been merely admiring from a distance for her whole time at university so far. She was beginning to understand the conversations that she had had with her girlfriends about that feeling of complete attraction, and her tummy was doing that fuzzy thing that Jas had described. She said it was what determined whether she liked the current bloke she was sleeping with or whether he would be another one-night stand to add to her ever-growing list. Jas was Mary's best friend at university, but they had big differences in morals.

Mary scanned the menu for a substantial yet not too bloating meal, but she was safe because with her cleavage being on show it meant that the bottom half of her top was flowy so would hide any bulges. She opted for a penne pasta dish with roasted peppers and a tomato sauce. She felt solid in her decision because it would give her energy to last through any body exerting activities that the rest of the day entailed. Who knew what they were going to get up to, and she was very excited for it. James proved his manly ways and chose the double bacon and cheeseburger which came out looking even grander than it sounded.

The conversation was still flowing about university and how things were going as well as home life but, thankfully, not too much about the past. Mary was rather shady about her past and preferred to enjoy whatever the future was to bring. If the future brought her more of James, then he was bound to hear it all, but for the time being she wanted to get stuck into her pasta so that the beer didn't take over and cause havoc before they had even started. Not that she'd had an overly bad past; she just didn't like to dwell on things in order to remain in her happy state which was a hugely celebrated element of her personality.

After they'd finished their meal and both felt sufficiently stuffed, they decided to move on to the next pub which wasn't hard to find in York, there were hundreds that lay within the city walls.

They headed to Kings Square and walked across diagonally in an attempt to avoid most of the more unlevelled streets of the city centre but including The Shambles in their route, the crooked famous street to add an element of cuteness to their date. They were on their way to the river because though the temperature felt cool, and more so having been sat by the cosy fire for half an hour warming their bones, the sun was shining, so it was nice to look out from inside a variety of bars. It certainly was going to be a variety as Mary was telling James on their walk to The Kings Arms about the many pub crawls that York had to offer and suggested trying one later. He was all for it which she liked realising that he too had a wild side and thoroughly enjoyed a drink.

'I'm having a really lovely day,' Mary exclaimed, feeling more gooey and confident now three pints down and onto the shorts.

James produced his gorgeous smile in agreement and took Mary's hand. She was pleased to have remembered to put on her mother's ring because it made her skinny, spindly and exceedingly long fingers look more feminine and attractive.

The ring glimmered as the sun shone on it, creating an image which mirrored how the two of them felt. Maybe love at first sight really did happen, Mary thought. Though she had waited a very long time to experience it. Twenty years old, and this was the first time she'd had these feelings, but these feelings were worth the long process, and she was very glad that James had been bold enough to ask her out on a date else she'd have probably reached forty before anything happened.

They entered the Kings Arms which hardly had any decoration; only marks on the walls acknowledging where the water reached the last time it flooded and a few photos depicting the same thing. It was the first time Mary had been in the pub in a sober enough state to notice this, but she found it rather interesting now that she was.

'Same again?' James asked Mary who was still taking in the surroundings of the cosy pub and seating herself in the corner on a wooden seat that turned out to be comfier than it looked.

'Yes please,' Mary replied in a spaced-out tone while her focus was on the dramatic flood pictures as well as her mother's ring and the emotions that came with it.

He brought the drinks over to where Mary sat and produced his smile that she knew would win her over many times in the future. They sat side by side on the bench, and James placed his hand gently on the top of her thigh, rubbing it compassionately. No words were being spoken, but it was as if they could already read one another's mind to know that they were both perfectly content in each other's company.

While the thoughts had been flowing around Mary's head, she realised that the silence had continued for the duration of their first drinks, and that they had been sitting and enjoying the moment, gazing into each other's eyes like a love scene from a film. Quickly snapping back into reality, Mary went to the toilet to check her makeup situation and to slightly lower her top to entice James to some drunken action later, or perhaps just a kiss. James went to the bar for another round.

'She really likes you,' uttered the barman with more experience in years than James had. 'You can tell from the way she holds herself around you. I've been watching the pair of you, not to sound creepy like, but it's cute.'

The barman was Geordie and had the strongest accent that he had heard since moving up north to university. He was short and bald, so James wrongly judged and thought what does he know, but he remained polite despite his inner judgement.

'I'm glad it looks that way,' he replied and swiftly moved on to the ordering of more drinks. There was an offer on spirits and mixers meaning Mary had been getting two drinks each time, so James made sure that he had two as well so not to feel left out. He remained on pints and didn't feel overly drunk yet, so he knew he couldn't get the blame for taking advantage of her or not acting in a gentlemanly manner and forgetting to walk her home, thoughts coming from experience.

He sat back at the table feeling smug with their beverage layout as well as hearing the comments from the barman proving that he was doing a good job. He'd never been so nervous on a date before, but so far he felt that his nerves were well hidden, and the attraction between the two of them was there.

After chatting a while more and opening up with the alcohol kicking in, they realised that they had more in common than they had initially thought. Even though Mary was the least sporty person and James had no interest for English literature and writing, they found lots of topics which meant something to them both and spent a good amount of time comparing travel notes which was full of laughter.

Once they'd finished the round and stood up ready to move on, Mary built up the courage to lean in for a kiss. She had never thought that she would let her guard down enough to do that on a first date before, but her feelings and mild intoxication made it happen. It was a comfortable moment as she leant into James' strong body. He held her hair back with one hand and grabbed her waist with the other, pinching it gently and affectionately tickling her on the ribs. She giggled, and after that moment they decided against the pub crawl and bought beverages to consume back at his flat.

Chapter 3
March 1994

It had been three weeks since the perfect day followed by the perfect night, and Mary couldn't get him off her mind. She had heard that the first time was always going to draw her in and make her think that he was the one, but she felt that, being an older starter, it was different. She was still shocked that she had let it happen since it was their first date, and it could be said the first time that they properly met, but being best friends with Jas who took the promiscuous reputation on her chin, Mary felt much happier about her fluidity in the moment.

She kept falling into a trap of fantasy when her mind wandered which happened far too frequently for her liking but then soon snapped back into reality remembering that she hadn't heard from James since. She had seen him a few times around the university grounds, but nothing had been said between them. Mary wasn't too worried, though, because her project was engulfing all of her time which meant that she was hardly in university but rather doing group work around each other's houses. This meant having a few books open and designating somebody as the writer who posed with a pen in their hand and a pad to lean on while they watched *Heartbeat* or opened a bottle of wine and chatted until the early hours.

The tameness of the assessment period on the social side was why Jas and Mary had made a point of venturing out into the city drinking one Saturday evening which they had been planning for weeks. They never usually planned nights out at the university and lived a spontaneous social life of going out most nights but deciding to do so half an hour before leaving the house. However, with the project and Jas's exam revision taking over for the past month they had set the date aside when it was all over and got as many people to join them to celebrate.

Mary was as late as ever getting ready, and Jas was getting agitated as they had agreed to meet everyone at The Junction at half past seven. It was already a quarter to, and Mary was laying on her bed in her dressing gown, though granted she had showered.

'Come on, Maz, you told me this wouldn't happen. You're late for everything, but this is the first time we've been out in ages, and you'll never be ready in time.'

'Oh, chill out and get a beer down you, will you? I'll be ready; I'm just relaxed at doing so.'

'Yeah, too chilled for my liking, do you want a beer?'

'That'd be lovely, darling. Mwah.'

Jas walked off smiling, knowing that she could never get angry at Mary, it was just her way. She had a personality with so many irritating characteristics to it that never fully irritated anybody because she would laugh it off or do something lovely a while later, and all would be forgotten.

After about fifteen minutes in the kitchen chatting to Sam who was heading home for a few days and just leaving, Jas returned to Mary's room to find her in exactly the same position as she was when she left. She handed her the beer and demanded that she got a move on as they were now definitely going to be late. With that authority, Mary finally got up into a vertical position and began the dramatic rush which happened each time she had to leave the house. Jas put on a *Fleetwood Mac* CD to liven the mood and inspire Mary to hurry up, and the girls laughed and danced while getting ready for the night.

Jas was obsessively watching her clock, though the beer had calmed her anal ways slightly, and she noticed that it was seven twenty-three, but by some miracle, as was always the case with Mary, Mary was fully clothed, made up and ready to go.

'Jas, have you got my keys?'

'Who cares where your keys are? I've got a set, and we'll be coming home together.'

'Not likely with your reputation but as soon as you leave the bar with whoever you choose tonight, make sure you hand me your keys, deal?'

'Deal!' Jas said this with a smirk, and just as they left the house, the phone started to ring.

The girls never got phone calls on a Saturday night because the only people who rang were their families who knew never to ring on a Saturday night because they were usually out. They were usually out most nights, so phone calls were mostly taken in the daytime while they were pretending to work or suffering badly from a hangover. Never at night.

Mary thought about the potential of the phone call being James. Perhaps he was asking her out for another date, and it had taken him the two-week waiting period to build up the courage. But then again, she knew that he had courage, and he had acted so smoothly during their time together that that explanation would be very out of character.

While Mary had been thinking up, shutting down all the possible solutions to James' absence and wondering whether that was a call from him, desperately wishing she could return quick enough to answer it without Jas knowing, Jas had noticed her silence.

'What's up with you? Thinking about that boy?' she asked with a variety of tones to her voice as if taking the micky, which Mary knew she was. 'Get over him and get under somebody else tonight, that's my motto.' Mary laughed, and for the first few minutes since that magical night she didn't think about James at all.

Everybody had moved on from The Junction to Cross Keys by the time the girls arrived which they were happy about because it was a livelier pub. The bar staff around the city knew the group well so would always let them know of people's whereabouts. However, with this knowledge, it didn't stop Jas and Mary acting oblivious for half an hour to take advantage of the cheap shot and pint deals for students at

The Junction. It was the only reason they started their nights there.

'Seriously, love, stop thinking about him,' Jas remarked to Mary when she went vacant again. 'Let's have a blast tonight, and we can figure it all out tomorrow. Here, one more shot, and then we'll go and meet the others.'

Mary took the shot glass and smiled to Jas as they clinked the two glasses together to cheers away the stress of exams. Mary loved Jas's attitude to most things in life. She had difficulty agreeing with her sexual habits, though they provided entertainment on days when she was feeling a bit down, but with everything else, Jas could usually think up a solution. She would be the first to see light in a god-awful situation, and she was good at brushing off hurtful words exchanged between them occasionally when things got too much. She was a great friend to have, and Mary leaned on her when needed, though she didn't rely on anyone much.

Having necked the shots and finished their pints, the girls headed to the Cross Keys feeling a little tipsy. They welcomed their tipsiness with open arms as the first person that they bumped into on entering the pub was Jamie, Jas's latest lover. The last that she had an amount of regret for anyway. Mary knew this instantly as she was never usually embarrassed when she bumped into any of her flings, but her face looked mortified. Having exchanged a few awkward words with him not to be rude, they went and found the people that they actually liked.

That was another reason that Mary was so fond of Jas because they were very particular with whom they spent time with. In fact, they didn't like many people at all, but that was okay because those that they did all had a similar mindset, so they had each other, and they were very content with that.

Mary couldn't stop her mind wandering to James and whether it was him on the phone. She was annoying herself and could sense that the girls had noticed her vacantness as she stared around the pub clocking every guy that passed and might have been him.

Perhaps he was at home wondering why she didn't pick up and whether he had lost his chance. Perhaps he had gone the other way and come out in rebellion, so if she bumped into him then he would be too drunk to talk sense with anyway. Maybe she was entirely wrong, and he didn't care for her much at all. During the moment of mindless wandering, she noticed how much more of their pints the rest of the group had drank than she had, so she picked hers up almost downing it to catch up.

'Woah, girl. Thirsty, are we?' Jas asked.

'I went into a day dream then panicked because you were all ahead.'

That never happened. Mary was a true Irish girl when it came to drink and always outdrank the group who were considered heavy drinkers for the English. It was a running joke, and if anybody survived a night out longer than Mary, then they were crowned champion, but it rarely happened.

Sometimes her dad would come up from London, and the girls would take him round the pubs of York. The first time he came, Jas, being the mouthy one, was claiming that she would take him under her wing and look after him in the madness of York's drinking culture. Little did she know that he was more advanced than Mary, in fact he had taught Mary everything that she knew, and after a few pints in he made the girls feel old and unable to keep up with his madness.

'The next round is my shout,' Mary declared as she finished the last dregs of her pint quicker than the rest who were ahead thirty seconds ago.

She quickly rose from her seat with a stronger mindset than before, and she squeezed in at the bar so the staff could see that she wanted to be served.

'Steady on love,' said one of the guys that she'd pushed in beside in jest. Mary gave him a confused look. 'I'm only joking, I've been served. Go ahead.'

'Thanks pet,' she declared, stating unintentionally, obviously her strong Irish accent and dialect which was instantly picked up on by the man the other side of her.

'Hey, Mary!' he remarked with a huge hint of jolliness in his voice. 'I've been hoping to bump into you for days.'

It was Mark, James' best friend, and Mary quickly scanned around the bar to see if James was out but hoped that she didn't seem too desperate to see him.

'He's not joined us, he was worried he'd bump into you,' Mark said as if answering her unasked question.

'Why would he not want to see me?'

'He thought he'd scared you off last time so was embarrassed to see you again. He figured no contact was a bad sign.'

'I've been thinking the same. Besides, how was I meant to contact him? He never gave me his number.'

Mark shrugged while being summoned by the boys to continue their pool tournament, so Mary figured that that was all she was going to get from him that night. She was left dazed and confused and was glad to see Jas coming over to help her carry the beers to the table.

'You all right? You look a bit worried?' Jas asked, concerned. 'Can we talk outside for a minute?'

Mary paid for the round, and they took everything to the table before heading outside for a cigarette chat. These were the best kinds of chats, Mary always thought, and the points in nights out when the most random topics of conversations came up and the biggest laughs were had. Chats during which the topic could range between anything from a bit of trivial gossip between friends right back to World War I and the real reason why it started, assessed through drunken mindsets and the haze caused by Mayfair Original.

Regardless of the fact that Mary enjoyed these talks, she had never experienced a troubled relationship type of chat, or rather never been on this end of one. She had heard her friends talk plenty about their relationship issues, and she'd always nodded in agreement when in fact she didn't have a clue. But this time she was beginning to relate about the difficulty in understanding the male race.

'I just don't know what to think, and Mark didn't give much away at all,' Mary said in a worried tone while removing the cigarette from her mouth and puffing out the smoke.

The girls didn't technically smoke at all, only socially, and usually when Jas wanted Mary's opinion on whether the guy she had her eye on in the bar would turn out to be another sleaze. That was why they always shared a cigarette because it didn't feel so bad that way, and they wouldn't regret it so much the next morning when they could taste it on their breath.

'Guys don't know anything about this stuff; they're worse than girls, so just ignore it. Besides, he said James was waiting on contact, right?'

'Yeah, I guess so, I just don't know where to go from here and wish he was out so I could speak with him.'

'I'll get his number off Mark, and we'll ring him tomorrow. For now though, let's have fun and find me a shag for tonight.'

Mary loved Jas's female dominance, and how she could take control of any situation even if it wasn't her own. The girls finished their cigarette and headed back to the table to join the others who were now onto the third round, with two extra pints waiting for Jas and Mary. A vision that both girls loved to see.

For a moment, Mary forgot all of the confusion between her and James and indulged in the present moment, never wanting her university days to end. She briefly thought in a mature manner noting that James may turn out to be just another short memory that she will look back on later in life with a smile. She realised that the girls she was sat with were the ones who would remain.

Having returned her focus back to the room and away from her thoughts, she noticed Jas was absent from the table. She saw her full pint remained in her place, so she began to worry about her whereabouts and scanned the bar. It turned out Jas quickly cottoned onto Mary's mind's unavailability in that instant and returned to the table a little while later with a tray of Sambuca shots.

'Girls night!' she shouted. 'We don't need any man.'

Jas often likened herself to Janis Joplin because her mum was an avid fan, so she grew up with the music and some of the sentences she came out with could have sounded just like Janis if she didn't have such a strong Yorkshire accent. Mary agreed with her, though, and the shots had the power to temporarily remove James from her mind.

Mary woke up to the phone ringing, and before she cursed it and thought how early it was to be ringing on a Sunday morning, she checked the time. It was half past eleven, and she was in Jas's bed feeling rotten and desperately hungover. She wondered whether Jas had chosen Mary's bed for last night's antics and desperately hoped not. She answered the phone quickly and hoped that it was James but realised that it was probably Jas.

'Girl, you're going to have to help me,' Jas pleaded on the other end of the phone.

'Where are you?'

'I'm at the lads.'

'I guessed that, but which lad is it this time? Give me a clue.'

'It's Mark, but before you lose it and refuse to come and retrieve me, I've got you a second date with James.'

With this information Mary leapt out of bed and flung on some clothes, quickly refreshed her mouth, sprayed perfume all over to help with her smoke and alcohol infused odour and practically ran to meet Jas at the corner of the lad's street. She was so intrigued.

If the romance didn't take place in the girls' flat which it often did and could hardly be classed as romance, then Jas usually phoned for rescue the next morning. Her vanity and sober dignity showed that she did care what others thought of her, and she didn't want to look so silly doing the walk of shame in last night's attire.

The girls briskly walked back, and Mary thought the whole way about the date with James feeling happy that he had agreed to meet again. Meanwhile, Jas was thinking how tactful her choice of bloke was last night choosing somebody who lived only a two-minute walk from their house which made her shameful walk far less agonising. Sometimes it was as if Mary had a very feminine brain and way of thinking, whereas Jas's was much more masculine and much less deep.

It was a strangely warm March day, so they chose to have a cup of tea outside, though both were dressed in big jumpers for warmth.

'Don't get too comfortable, Hun. He's coming to knock for you about two,' Jas said with her trademark smirk, knowing that she had gained even more respect from Mary, and that she would never be asked about the other guy she slept with before Mark last night. After all, even she was a little ashamed and embarrassed which she realised was a feeling that was becoming more frequent in her life.

Mary didn't care for the details on how Jas managed to organise date number two, she was too excited for it to bother with that. She didn't even want to know what they were doing to work on a suitable dress code, all she wanted was to see James, and she felt overwhelmed with relief that she wasn't that awful in bed that he had been put off entirely.

James was as punctual as he was the first time, and the doorbell went off at precisely two o'clock. Mary was for once on time through sheer excitement and didn't even say to Jas that she was leaving. As they walked hand in hand to the centre of York, Mary knew so strongly that James was the one. She wasn't sure what made her so confident, but she just knew they would marry one day.

Chapter 4
Dublin, 2018

I have woken up feeling as if last night was a huge blur though I wasn't drunk in the slightest. The queues for the bar were ridiculous, so a large glass of mint lemonade on our way to our seats was enough, but I look forward to the days when Erin can be my waitress that's for sure. The concert was so brilliant and halted my mind from wandering throughout which these days is a miracle. Sadly, lying in bed on a Saturday morning with two sleeping children isn't having the same brain numbing effect, and the Tinnitus isn't helping matters either. Oh, for the days when I would go to concerts and that was only the beginning of the night. After the concert was over, we'd all go out to bars and clubs, waking up the following day feeling fabulous and ready for the next round. How we managed, I fail to understand. How I ever obtained a degree is beyond me.

I suddenly feel very old, very alone, and I close my eyes trying to dream of happier circumstances. I am very happy in the company of my children who keep me going every day. Daddy helps too, but my mind drifts to times with James when he was still alive. The happiness that I felt each moment that I spent with him. Each time he kissed me. The moment he looked into my eyes with total pride at the birth of both of our children. When we'd be socialising, and he would gaze over to me with a smile showing sheer fulfilment to me being wholly his? I miss it all dreadfully.

This only leads me to obsess over the shock and hurt I felt the day it happened and the torment I went through for the following five years afterwards. A truly sad ending to nineteen years of marriage. A sad closure to what felt like a lifetime of friendship. I would never wish that on anyone.

I even think up times with Mammy and Daddy happily watching over me playing on the swing in our garden, or when Daddy used to toss me over his shoulder in McDintons and threaten me with the ice bucket. Mammy would always tell him off which was when I remember that she did have a hint of maternal instinct inside her stern frame.

I notice the sunshine peeping through the window and get up to open the curtains to let the day in. I consider whether it's too early for a beer to calm my busy head but then see that it's not even close to the sun being over the yardarm, even though we are in Dublin, so whether that rule counts or not I'm yet to decide. Not to mention my total avoidance of alcohol these days which sometimes I find incredibly boring, but it's something that I know I must stick with. I figure a cup of tea would be more appropriate, and on getting up to make myself one, Erin wakes and Jack merely stirs. Perfect, I think to myself, a nice brew with my lovely daughter, what better way to start the day.

Erin hasn't found her love for tea yet and opts for a glass of juice which she gulps while cuddled in beside me on the sofa looking out at the busy streets of Dublin. A peaceful moment during which I have a sudden urge to put the song *'Molly Malone'* on, changing the mood somewhat and sing my heart out to praise my Irish routes. I then realise that I'm no longer a completely stoned twenty something, and I must enjoy calm moments like this with my children. This is my life now.

We would have the television on, but I can't seem to work it and don't dare let Erin try for fear that she'll break it or the whole debacle will end in a huge row. We haven't yet started the rowing which is inevitable between mother and daughter during her teenage years, especially a child with the temperament that Erin is developing rapidly. However, I fear it won't be long, and the looks she gives me sometimes are deathly.

We look at each other and smile in contentment, while I think about what I can do with the children today to keep them entertained and keep my mind from drifting away. We've managed to enjoy the quiet for what has probably been ten minutes before Jack comes hurtling in pointing to his nose and describing, in broken sentences, but luckily, I have eyes to see, a nosebleed.

'Oh darling,' I say in a comforting tone, 'what's happened here?'

Small sobs come from his little face as I hold a tissue firmly on his nose while rubbing his back to reassure him that he will be fine. I know that he won't be crying out of pain but rather fear and worry as to what's happening to him and the inability to effectively communicate this. He has been through a lot in his short lifetime, and each time he has to deal with a new hurdle, I notice that he's getting stronger, even if it's by a miniscule amount. I realise that not many people would describe a small nosebleed as one of life's struggles, but for my Jack it's just another peculiar thing about this world that he has to understand.

The peace returns in our flat after the blood has been mopped up, Jack has been reassured, and another cup of tea has been consumed by me. I feel glad that we got the 48-hour bus ticket so that even if the first few hours of our day are spent sat on the top deck and enjoying one full trip around the city while I decide on something fun to do, the kids will still feel entertained and as if I know what I am doing. Surprisingly, Jack is ready first which prompts Erin and I to hurry, both realising that he will kick up a storm if he's sat waiting for too long. Something that both of us could do without.

I think of the old days in Dublin and how I'd have spent my time here if I'd have stayed. A good twenty years would have been guzzled up in Temple bar drinking the pricey beverages in between whatever job I'd have got. It certainly wouldn't have been teaching that's for sure. Though I suppose York's drinking culture isn't dissimilar in terms of the number of pubs to choose from and the time at which the locals deem

41

it acceptable to begin drinking, so perhaps I would have managed a degree if I'd have stayed after all. I wish I'd have brought James here at least once, but we never had a reason, and I never had a desire to visit. Aunt Eileen always came to us, she liked England, and nobody else was worth the hassle.

Thankfully, we timed the walk to the bus stop perfectly, and a green bus pulled up as soon as we arrived which Jack got highly excited about in his own unique way. Erin had her earphones at the ready, and on my apparently ridiculous suggestion of listening to the commentary to learn something new, she shrugged and put the right one in her ear as a bold statement against my orders. Due to the blood episode earlier, we have left the flat a little later than intended which has meant that the top deck was almost full though two seats together are waiting for Jack and myself, while Erin has occupied one next to a smiley old man behind who warmly welcomes her anti-social self.

Off we go again, learning about the Spire of Dublin and the rebellion outside the Great Post Office during the Easter Rising in 1916. Scars of which can still be seen on the buildings in the form of bullet indents. This is something which I find shocking, Jack thinks is pretty cool and Erin is completely oblivious to. I think I'll keep Jack entertained later with a miniature quiz about the facts which I am sure he has taken on board throughout our time on the bus. He will be even more chuffed because there is no way that Erin will be able to beat him having likely retained no information at all.

The sun is out, and my water supply is depleting which fills me half with happiness for the glorious weather and half with frustration knowing that we will have to get off before the end of this loop to restock on fluids. I would love these fluids to be alcoholic, but then I kick myself remembering the company I am in, and that alcohol for me is something of the past.

I have always drunk too much but never felt I had a problem until James' injury when alcohol became a means of coping rather than enjoyment. That's what daddy has always said that I needed to decipher between. He said that when you find yourself turning desperately to drink to solve all your problems then it has become an issue and needs to be addressed. He's not reached that point so continues to enjoy a bottle of wine a night and more if he's socialising with friends which is a frequent occurrence. He calls wine the fixer of all things bad, but still claims he is completely in control. Questionable.

I decided to cut it out fully back in May 2016, just before James and I separated. Things were at their highest level of crazy, and I realised that the drink wasn't solving anything nor helping me to get through it. In fact, it was only making matters worse, and after a strict talking to from a physician, I packed the booze in and feel no better nor worse for doing so. To be totally honest right now, I could enjoy a tasty cider in the sunshine, and if I was away with adults I probably would. Cider isn't strong; I used to use it as a break in between the stronger spirits, as a means of sobering myself up a little on heavy nights out. I always said from the minute I gave up that it wouldn't necessarily be forever just for now. I've got McDinton blood, quitting alcohol is never going to be forever.

As predicted, our water supplies have run out, but we are close to stop number sixteen which is right in the centre of the city, so the choice of cafés and shops is vast. We pass a small newsagent which looks like an inviting place to grab some drinks from before a walk along the river. I smile when looking around to see Taytos and plain bread on the shelves which reminds me instantly of Mammy's packed lunches for school or when she palmed me off to a friend so she could enjoy a child free night in the pub. A nostalgic smile appears on my face.

I try to make out what Jack is asking me, but his speech has diminished even more recently, so this proves a very tricky task. Occasionally, he will utter a sentence as clear as he used to sound, but then he goes back to communicating via body language and the odd grunt, and I have to concentrate intensely. Over time I have learnt to make sense of Jack's unique way of communicating, and we have been known to have full conversations, but it is a very difficult matter to come to terms with. Particularly because he was an extraordinarily early speaker and built a strong ability to communicate, so when it vanished entirely another part of me broke. Especially because the trauma was largely to blame, so in my warped mind that blame should be on me.

Erin never assists the situation which I have to remember she can't help because it's hard for her to understand as well. She gets frustrated, failing to see why her brother at the age of eight has lost all abilities to speak, and she sees it as highly attention seeking. The doctors have explained the psychology behind it, but I don't fully comprehend it so cannot expect my fourteen-year-old daughter to grasp it at all.

I am pleased to see my children both grabbing a bag of Taytos each, so I too get one to keep us all going, and after paying the sweet girl behind the counter, we head off for a walk. I can't believe how lucky we have been with the weather for the past few days because Dublin is renowned for being wet. Again, my body fills with pure contentment, and I forget all about the scary intentions of this visit.

I look to my right to see that Erin has removed both headphones and is walking along holding onto Jack's hand, both smiling. It's a picture that I'd love to take if I knew how to use my phone properly, and I was standing a few steps behind so that they wouldn't notice, but I realise it is a memory that I'll just have to cherish within my head. The light breeze makes this moment even more enjoyable, and regardless of the dark motives that brought me here, I am grateful that we have come.

I can't believe how long that bus takes to get around, and we must have been walking for longer than I thought because I look at my watch to see it is lunchtime already. Luckily, we have been mooching around the centre, so I have spotted some nice places to eat on the way, noting their prices as always. Though I have thought to myself that with it being the penultimate day of our stay and predicting the stress I will go through tomorrow, I am happy to stretch the budget and enjoy. As we need to have a chilled night at the flat tonight because I have a heap of phone calls to make regarding tomorrows meet, I decide for a bigger lunch and pre-empt a snack like tea later.

A burger house catches Erin's eye, and keeping her happy is key today because she understands patches of the goings on tomorrow, and so I don't want her mood to make a difficult situation worse. In terms of eateries, Jack has always been easy, so the burger house is where we go, choosing a spot outside in the sun.

A poor lady sat on the table next to us with a screaming baby, and an older child in a foul mood makes me appreciate the ease of my two. They have their moments but nothing too drastic, and usually they give me the warm feeling of having done a fairly good job of bringing them up. Their manners are impeccable and something we have adamantly picked up on, so I always feel more pride when the waiter asks for their order and pleases and thank-yous follow everything that they say.

While relishing in the pride of my children, I scan the drinks menu, trying to avoid the alcoholic sections for fear I will crumble. I don't know what has got into me recently, but for the first time since I gave it up, the craving for an ice-cold Corona has become increasingly persistent. Or something much stronger now I think about it.

With thanks to the emphasis on the huge healthy eating cultures of present times, there is a wide selection of non-alcoholic mocktails which please my palette almost as much. I choose the Passion Fruit Explosion which is brought out to me full of colour and tasty fruit.

That same sense of pleasure hits me in this moment, and it's enhanced with the remembrance of Daddy coming to join us tomorrow. He'll be able to take the kids off my hands while I figure out what to do. I always feel excited to see my dad, and any time spent with him is special. His presence tomorrow will help matters no end regardless as to whether he has any advice or not.

Seeing that face yesterday was so unexpected and has now made me reconsider everything. The beaten eye, the pale skin, the thinness and worn out look made all my presumptions seem more plausible and has taken the strength from me altogether. Deep down, I expected exactly what I saw, but on the surface, I needed warning to cope.

I think to myself how long I still have to do this and whether now is the right time. Certainly, tomorrow won't be, so I figure I'll spend the day going through things and planning it all better next time. I can make something up, I'm good at excuses, and I just won't show. I'll return to York and write a letter rearranging for another date. The children won't question anything once the surprise of their granddad coming to visit and taking them out for the day is revealed.

My eyes move over to both of my children who are sitting opposite to me eating their meals with such innocence in their every move. I didn't recognise eating as an innocent act until now, but that is the only word that I can appropriately describe it with, especially considering all the malignant goings on inside my mind. If only they knew the emotions going through me right now, if only they were a lot older so I could offload a bit onto them. I instantly retract this thought and realise that it would never be fair to pile any of this onto them. They never need to be involved.

I think to myself whether I should waste my energy on the anger I can't help but feel towards her despite everything she has done for me. I wonder whether her mother is still alive with her tight jeans and leather jacket, roaming around as if still eighteen. I long for somebody else to be going through this with me, but even Daddy doesn't know the full picture, and I think things would be worse if he did.

Jack clocks on to my temporary absence and asks in the best English that I've heard since his voice disappeared if I am okay. I have never known how obvious it is when my mind goes off into the deep, unsolved past, but everybody I have ever met has been able to tell straight away.

'I am fine, honey, now finish your meal.'

I browse the restaurant considering whether I will ever find somebody else, even purely for companionship, not necessarily love. This is something that I have never thought about before, and it strikes me that perhaps I am now ready to move on. A man with dark hair looks over in our direction and smiles. I feel happy until I realise that he's only grinning at Jack's face covered in ketchup from taking huge bites of burger too large for his mouth. It is at this point when the motivation builds within me. It is at this point that I realise our stay in Dublin is going to have to last a lot longer than just one more day.

Chapter 5
Dublin, 1988

Moving to a new house was something that Mary had always been familiar with because her mother could never settle upon one place. The family didn't ever move far from Dublin because the pub remained a constant throughout Mary's childhood in Ireland, and it had been in the family for years, so selling was never an option for Anna and Séan. However, to onlookers it would have seemed as if Anna's mission was to occupy every house at some point within a five-mile radius of the city.

McDintons acted as Mary's safe space as she always found it confusing and somewhat unsettling upping and leaving house after house. It took her until ten years old to discover that perhaps the explanation was as shallow as her mother always wanting a project on the go and getting bored easily once the next house had been completed. Ten years old was too late to discuss this issue though, so she guessed she would never know.

Anna loved interior design and changed the pub's décor almost monthly, but it could never be said that she wasn't talented as the place always looked beautiful. She would pick a colour scheme and put everything into it with a few quirks added to make it unique, and then a few weeks down the line the boredom would kick in, and her mind would be buzzing with new ideas to revamp it all. It was a trait that Séan became increasingly irritated by and failed to understand about his wife, yet it was one of the few things that Mary adored about her mother.

Her mother's itchiness was the reason why a huge move to London leaving everything behind, McDinton's included, didn't prove overly difficult for Mary. At fourteen, she was to leave her family, her friends, her school, her safe place and start all over again in a foreign environment. They wouldn't even have the same accent, she thought, as she packed the last of her things into the bag that she was to take with her on the flight. That's what her daddy had told her: one big suitcase that goes under the plane, and one small bag that comes on the plane with you.

This was another thing that was going to be new. She had never flown before, and apart from a few weekends with her Aunt, she had hardly gone away from Dublin and everything she knew so well. One thing that she knew would help her through the upheaval of life as she knew it was that being in the reassuring company of her father would eradicate all her worries.

She had been quite excited about the new adventure for the weeks leading up to it, and it wasn't until they had checked in and were sat at the departure gate that the nerves kicked in. Séan had gone to the bar and had Mary mind the seats and belongings when she began to run through everything in her mind. The world had never seemed a big place until that moment, and she had always been quite content with her lot without fear over what the future held. Even after losing her mother at such a young age, and under such dire circumstances almost having to accept a stand in Mum immediately after didn't faze her in ways that it would most young girls.

Suddenly, all the emotions she should have felt a few months back came rushing into her all at once. She felt angry towards her dad but understood why he did it. She felt sad for him too and sad for her mother's death. She even felt slightly sorry for Sheila, but that feeling only lasted a minute or two before it turned to rage. Most of all, she felt terrified to be going to England and to be going forever.

Séan returned with his beer and a glass of Cola for Mary. He always had a smile on his face, particularly in her company, and for that she loved him more. He would never spoil Mary, but she knew how to get exactly what she wanted, and they shared a bond that any fourteen-year-old girl would be jealous of. Holding on to the closeness between them was the only thing stopping Mary from throwing a toddler like tantrum and demanding that they didn't get on the flight. Séan could sense her anxieties, though, and gently placed his arm around her as she sipped happily on her drink. She winced as some bubbles entered her nostrils.

The departure lounge was full of what Mary quite maturely observed as the hidden parts of life. By this she meant that whenever someone records their holiday, they will never describe the uncomfortable wait at the departure gate with two screaming kids and a very miserable husband. They'll never remark on the cost of food and drink which is only able to happen because everybody is trapped, thirsty and hungry so they have no choice but to pay the extortionate prices. They will fail to acknowledge the uneasiness that they have for the flight ahead, and how no amount of scientific comprehension will ever convince them that a lump of metal the weight of a plane can remain in the air. Mary watched this scene with a slight smirk illustrating her thoughts, and for an instant she forgot her turmoil of emotions which was whirring around her a moment ago and remained in the present.

She noticed her dad's beer level rapidly lowering down the glass and hoped he wouldn't get drunk before they got on the flight. As much as she loved him, his drinking habits occasionally became embarrassing which was usually fine because they would be in McDinton's, but in public she prayed that he would act normal.

'What? It's the last decent pint I'll be having,' Séan remarked, spotting Mary watching his glass.

He said it with a friendly tone, and Mary laughed knowing that he would be having another beer on touch down in England, innocently unaware that Guinness was apparently never the same away from Ireland.

Sat right in front of the board, they knew which gate to go to as soon as it was displayed, and with Mary's nerves, she urged her dad to finish his pint as soon as this information was available. This was the only part of the procedure that Mary remembered from her dad's explanation the night before about what to expect. She had forgotten the passport checks, but luckily, he took control of that, and she had no idea what the plane would look like, let alone what to imagine at the other end.

The concept of flying was just about the only thing that didn't fill her with fear but just about the only thing that worried Séan, though he did a good job of acting calm the whole way. As they stood in the long queue of excitable holidaymakers, she tried to mask her fears with the fact that around half an hour later she would be flying above the clouds, and that fascinated her.

She wondered how high up they would go, and what she would be able to see. She pictured birds flying past the window and smiling in at her to ease her worries. Then she remembered that birds can't smile, they didn't have teeth. She contemplated the speed at which they would take off and how this process would work.

She had seen one plane take off in her lifetime, but she couldn't remember why seeing as she had never been on one. She thought perhaps it was a small biplane at an airfield she had been to because she couldn't remember going to an airport before either. It must travel extremely fast, she thought, as the airhostess checked their passports and wished them a safe flight.

She questioned what the food would be like but kept those thoughts inside her head not to seem greedy as she knew her dad would think she was. As much as he loved her and rarely said a negative thing around her, Mary's dad had a huge demand for being grateful. He said that everyone in life always wants more and is never thankful for what they have, and he drilled this notion into Mary almost daily so that she thought that way too.

She didn't even know how big the plane would be or what it would look like inside. Then, while walking down the narrow corridor to the outside airfield, she chuckled at her obliviousness. She didn't know a thing.

Glancing at her ticket and trying to subtly peer over at her father's, she tried to see what seat number he had to make sure that they would be sitting next to each other. She had always been confident in stranger's company and would describe herself as a friendly person. Growing up in the surroundings of McDintons she couldn't be any other way, and her parents would often sit her with the guests who were willing to entertain a young child so that they could get on with running the place. She didn't know why suddenly this comfort had lifted, and she felt terrified to be slowly moving along towards a plane full of people that she had never met before. In fact, all of her personality traits seemed to have been replaced with the opposition during the move, and she was worried that they would never return.

'Are you okay, darling?' Séan said, realising that Mary felt uneasy.

'Yeah,' she replied quietly, hiding every emotion inside her head.

This was something she had become extremely good at, and nobody knew she was doing it. The people around her just thought she was incredibly strong for a girl her age who had been through everything she had. She was always okay with this and didn't want anybody to know how she really felt because then she would be bombarded with questions to which she had no answer. At least, no answer that she wanted to give.

'Good afternoon, sir and madam, your seats are six rows up on the left. You, my dear, can sit by the window,' The air hostess said this with a grin on her face and Mary didn't understand why.

She had no intention of sitting by the window and no knowledge as to why this would provoke such an excited expression upon the airhostesses' faces. A fear of heights was something that Mary hadn't yet had the chance to discover because she had never partaken in any activity that involved being really high up. She hoped that this phobia would remain undiscovered because the emotions going through her were too much to handle, she couldn't cope with real fear as well.

The plane, though a bit stuffy, was pleasant, and the seats were more comfortable than she had expected. Séan was sitting beside her, and next to him was a friendly man who, of course, Séan had instigated fluffy conversation with. He had a tendency to do this wherever he went which Mary loved because it broke any ice remaining and immediately evaporated any bleak vibes, which had often been created when her mother was involved.

It was the type of conversation which didn't mean much but flowed as if the two people had known each other forever. His conversation was full of wit, and he usually had people in stitches from the offset. This man was no different, and Mary felt thankful listening to their exchange of meaningless remarks that all her worries had vanished temporarily.

The engine had been running the whole time they had been on board, but Mary looked up from the magazine she was glancing through to see that the aircraft had begun to move slowly. It better speed up, she thought, if there was any chance of them having lift off. Bored from the slowness, she returned to the magazine to look at lunch options but subtly as ever so Séan wouldn't notice. A cheese and chutney sandwich took her fancy as did the pricey perfumes on the pages before.

She hadn't been allowed much in terms of cosmetics so far in life. Her dad wanted to keep her pure and let makeup wait for the time being. However, she had recently started to take an interest in it, and browsing was one of her favourite things to do.

Time passed by, and her mind was focussed enough on the products to keep it away from horrible thoughts, while at the same time, reading was still a relaxing thing to do. This time seemed to be a little different which was why she had moved on to look at food options. The perfumes made her think of her mother and how she had never kept anything that would remind her of the memories in the future. Most girls would keep an item of jewellery or purchase their mother's token perfume on loop, but Mary had opted for stale memories soaked in bad taste, and for a second, she was beginning to regret this decision. She then remembered the ring her dad had saved for her, but she wasn't allowed to wear it until she turned eighteen, so by that point she would probably have forgotten about it anyway.

'Would everybody please take the time to read the safety cards in front of them which should explain anything that was unclear in the demonstration,' came the voice from above, and Mary realised that she had been glued to the magazine throughout the entire show whatever it had been.

She had a tendency to space out like this and become completely oblivious to all that was going on around her. The important demonstration which included some vital information clearly wasn't going to be different. Oh well, she thought, if I die, I die.

She had always wanted to see airhostesses at work and wondered how in sync their safety briefings were. She imagined it would be like a dance routine only slower and without music. All imagination aside, she guessed she would have to wait until they got on another flight to see for herself and remember to watch that time. Anyway, she predicted strongly that this would be a long while away because her dad would want to stay put in London after the turmoil of their last few years in Ireland.

Unsure as to whether or not they would ever return to Ireland, nothing luring them in other than the homely feel, she hoped that the continent would be their next port of call for a visit, a place which, of course, they would fly to. Spain or France would do just somewhere different and exciting, but she wasn't going to make any suggestions to her dad just yet, worried that she would sound incredibly spoilt and he would probably tell her that she was.

The engine suddenly picked up, and the only association Mary had to the noise it was making was that it sounded like the sea which brought her comfortably back home. How you could feel at home on board a plane shaped piece of tin manoeuvring around a dull concrete space, she had no clue, but at home is what she felt. The sound of the sea comforted her wherever she was and took her to a place that she loved. She didn't quite know where this place was, and the image inside her mind was a little blurry, but it was a good place nonetheless containing all of her happy memories which she had sifted out from the bad. The moment she heard anything that resembled the waves crashing into shore she would be gone for a while and peacefully so.

Her seat shaking as if on a bumpy road brought her swiftly back into reality, and she knew quite confidently that this was going to be take off. The moment she had been waiting for in anticipation and a moment which had seemed to take forever to reach, the impatient fourteen-year-old that she was.

The noise increased in volume, and the movement began while Mary looked out of the window, intrigued as to how it would all work. How a weighty plane would be able to fly them to England. How they would even get it off of the ground to begin with.

She didn't know that she would be as afraid as she was during this stage of the flight, but she couldn't stop herself gripping tightly onto the seat and sitting upright and leaning backwards as if somebody was behind her about to push and she was stood on a cliff edge. Séan put his hand upon hers to reassure her, and she looked up at him to share the smile.

As the plane lifted off the ground Mary's nerves settled, and she felt thankful that she wouldn't spend the entire flight gripping onto her seat prompting something awful to happen. The clouds looked false from up above like a sea of marshmallows that you could jump on if you tried. She watched as her home became smaller and noticed the world becoming bigger when she looked up through her tiny circular window to see a never-ending sky of blue.

At last they were off. Off into the sky, over the ocean and heading to London. They were leaving everything that she ever knew behind apart from her beloved dad and the memories which she was always good at keeping close to her to use as a comfort blanket when needed.

Chapter 6
London, 1988

Mary's eyes slowly opened to a crash onto the ground. Her dad looked down to her, smiling as if to assure her that everything was going to be okay, and she wasn't sure if the look was meant for clarity in the current moment or in general.

'We're here now, darling,' he said with a warmer voice than the weather looked outside the small round window of the aeroplane.

She hadn't known what to expect of England, but from first impressions she could see that the weather conditions were no improvement to what she had left back at home.

Thankfully, the crash was a safe landing onto the tarmac of Stansted Airport, and there was nothing for Mary to panic about other than the alienation, separation and a complete restart of her life in a place that she didn't know nor knew anybody in it. Other than that, she would be fine. She was feeling surprisingly calm and followed her dad's actions entirely, grabbing her bag and heading to the exit doors of the aircraft.

The chill hit her straight away while descending the slippery steps, implying that it had been raining, and she thought to herself that actually England had worse weather than Ireland, and the people didn't seem too friendly either. In fact, the only thing making the trip worthwhile so far was her dad standing beside her, but she realised that it was too early to judge.

Séan's total lack of organisation made her chuckle as she watched him flap around searching through the contents of his rucksack in attempt to find their passports and visas to allow them entry to the UK on a long-term basis. She still didn't understand her father's choice of London for their place of residency, seeing as no family lived in England, and they were both quite happy in Ireland before everything went on. No family that she knew of anyway. She didn't grasp why the circumstances led them to flee. In her opinion, everything would have passed, and they would have been happy after it had, happier still, remaining in their home place which they loved. However, she wasn't going to ask any of those sorts of questions just yet, especially as her dad was becoming more and more stressed unable to locate the documents.

They waded their way through the reams of pointless rope which guided people to queue in an orderly fashion, yet there weren't any people to guide, so it seemed a waste. Eventually, they reached the back of the queue, and Mary could tell already that this was going to be a long day.

'Daddy, where are we actually going to be living?' she asked shocked that she hadn't thought of that part yet.

'I have an old friend in Chiswick. He has said we can stay a while until we find our feet.' His voice sounded uncertain, but Mary guessed that this was due to his concentration being distracted on the documents.

Mary assumed that her dad had no English friends due to the amount that he ridiculed them daily, but she asked no more questions and prayed for the queue to reduce in size. She didn't know what they were queuing for and hadn't got a clue as to what was going to happen when they became the first people in queue, but she trusted her dad, and he seemed to know what he was doing.

'Next please, sir. Are you two together?' asked the friendly gentleman at the desk.

Mary found his accent quite comical and had never heard someone sound so posh before. Maybe that's how the Queen sounds along with all the other members of the royal family, she thought.

Séan presented their passports and spoke some jargon with the man, none of which Mary understood, but it was obviously good talk because they were allowed through to the conveyer belts which would bring their luggage. She only gathered this because the signs read *baggage claim* all over the place. Séan had obviously done this before, Mary assumed, as he had got a metal trolley on which to carry everything. Always thinking ahead was her father, and always finding ways to make life easier.

She could see signs everywhere, and arrows and exits. There were members of staff stood around not doing much at all and others who looked rushed off their feet, so she wondered why they didn't get better at sharing the workload. The first bag came around the corner, and a very happy couple grabbed it finding it hilarious that they didn't have to wait and could beat the traffic queues. Mary hoped that the smug couple's car battery had run down like it had on her mum's car when they were due to go to her gran's once or that they couldn't find their keys. Then she silently had a word with herself for being so cynical as they were probably lovely people, she was just bored of walking, then waiting, then walking so much.

Once they had grabbed their bags and Séan had figured out taxi numbers and prices with the very helpful lady in the tourist information centre, they headed to the rank for another waiting episode during which Mary observed maturely the goings on around her. She often did this, and anybody who she openly spoke to about what she perceived would tell her that she has an old head. She never knew what they meant by this expression but nodded and continued her inspections.

The taxi driver was very nice, but he too had that funny accent the same as the man on the passport desk. The taxi was also something new, and one thing about England that she had seen photographed—the black cab. She couldn't remember where she had seen it and gathered that tourist shops in Ireland wouldn't be promoting very English memorabilia, but she had definitely seen a picture of the famous British feature. She thought it was surreal to be witnessing the reality of these vehicles and cooler still to be travelling inside one.

Mary had always felt that the traffic was bad in Dublin, but London trumped Dublin's busiest times. For the entire journey all Mary heard was the beeping of horns from angry drivers. She found it funny to watch the anger show all over their faces and in the dramatic hand gestures which were sometimes quite rude. What all the fuss was about she didn't know, nor could she understand why people thought that making this commotion inside your car would help the traffic move more smoothly.

Luckily, the two of them were in no rush, so the traffic was okay. It will be different when her dad begins to work, she noted. A train of thought entered her head which made her wonder what her dad was planning to do for work over in London, and whether he had sold McDintons or kept it in case they decided to move back home.

All of these questions she stored away for a later date because she felt it too soon to be bombarding her dad with them. Besides, for all she knew he could be feeling quite nervous too.

She couldn't believe how absorbed in the goings on back home she had been not to notice conversations about the pub or her dad's work. She was used to listening in on her parent's conversations, always wanting to know absolutely everything, but without her mum she figured that no conversation was interesting enough for her to care about anymore.

The chat between her dad and the taxi driver was pretty boring in Mary's opinion which was why her mind was focussed on other topics. She hadn't been in many taxis in her lifetime because mostly they spent their free time in the city; if they had gone away it would have been with an auntie or her parents, so they would have taken the car. She did remember in the few taxi rides she'd had there were similarly dull discussions during them though. It was full of what she thought was termed *small talk*. She'd never wanted to travel far if she was with her mother because she worried it would get awkward as her mum often ran out of things to say. Séan, on the other hand, never had this problem and was the king of this small talk which he was demonstrating in the current situation, the same as he did on the flight.

As they got closer to their destination which was unknown to Mary, the houses became larger and less cramped together. The tacky looking newsagents which were cropping up every other building before had vanished, and the dirty streets had become much cleaner. Some of the fronts of the buildings looked more like palaces than people's homes, and Mary wondered which one the Queen lived in. Perhaps it was one of those. Perhaps they were to be staying with a member of the royal family. She swiftly stopped those thoughts knowing with certainty that the Queen lived at Buckingham Palace and hoped that her dad would take her there quite soon.

Even though it had been drilled into her from a young age that she had Irish blood and the English were very much a separate entity, one thing she had always loved about England, from the little that she knew, was the royal family. She had watched Princess Diana and Prince Charles' wedding on her auntie's television during the summer holidays. She sat there for the whole day being fed ice cream and fruit but not moving her eyes from the box. Her aunt was having a party which most certainly was not in aid of the wedding, but Mary removed herself from this and was utterly absorbed by Dianna's beauty and the sheer Britishness of it all. She realised that this was going against all morals that her parents had taught her but, in that moment, she didn't care at all.

She could feel a slight cramp developing in her right foot and was glad to see that they were just arriving at the house. It was a very grand house, and she wondered how her dad knew such rich people. A man who Mary guessed was Séan's friend Derek was waiting on the porch steps waving happily in their direction. Though she couldn't help but feel there was a slight reserve in this happiness that he depicted, that something more sinister was underlying. Again, she inwardly slapped herself for passing too fast a judgement on the poor man.

The taxi pulled up to a set of iron gates that opened on cue. She was amazed that a house of that size could fit in the cramped London City and wondered whether she had fallen asleep and missed their drive out into the countryside where there is much more space. The driveway wasn't as long as she had imagined one would be with the gates they had just gone through, but the house was something she had never thought she would associate herself with.

She desperately wanted to know how her dad knew somebody so rich, and why they hadn't met before. He would have bought the most fantastic birthday presents and sent a ten euro note in her Christmas cards, she was sure of it. The most she ever received was a two-euro coin from Aunt Eileen which she appreciated with gritted teeth because Eileen usually watched her open the card. She quickly stopped herself knowing that if she was more vocal about what was going on inside her head then her dad would be mortified at her rotten thoughts.

Derek's friendly manner was obvious from the offset as he couldn't be happier to take their things and show them around his house, telling them the usual expressions to make themselves at home and so on. Mary suspected that Derek and her dad hadn't seen each other for years, as his reaction to her was one of shock when he saw how big she was. At least she thought it was shock, it could have been mistaken for animosity towards Séan, but she disregarded that thought questioning why Séan would have chosen to stay with somebody that he didn't like.

Maybe Derek was expecting Mary to be much younger than she was. Maybe her dad failed to mention that he had a child altogether. Whatever the situation was, Mary knew they had a lot to catch up on. She, quite frankly, had heard enough about it, so hoped that she would be able to sneak off to bed early.

During their tour of the fabulously large place that Derek and his wife called home, Mary spotted who she presumed was Derek's wife setting up the dining room for dinner. This was a sight that she was pleased to see because even though her plans of escape were quite real, she didn't want to go without food and couldn't remember the last time she had a decent meal inside her.

Though she blanked out what they were saying to each other, she hoped her meandering mind wasn't too obvious and that neither her dad nor Derek directed the conversation her way because she really hadn't been involved in any aspect of it during the tour. She knew she could appear to be fully involved in the conversation if she was asked a question because she was genuinely amazed by the house. Praising it would hopefully mask her mind's absence.

'So that's about it. Get yourselves sorted and we'll be down here with dinner whenever you're ready,' Derek said with nothing but genuine warmth in his voice.

'Thank you, I really appreciate you doing this for us,' Séan replied with sincerity.

'No bother, anytime.'

Having heard Derek's reply Mary thought for the first time that perhaps Derek wasn't an English friend of her dad's but rather an Irishman who had moved over just as they were doing.

Her dad led her to their beds which were luckily in rooms next door to each other because the size of the house made Mary certain that it would be scary at night. Knowing that she didn't have far to go to get to her dad gave her comfort.

As she entered the room which had only been pointed to briefly during the house introduction, she couldn't believe how perfect it was. It was decorated as if they had redesigned it especially for her arrival. The single bed in the middle of the back wall had pink sparkling curtains hanging down from the ceiling, something that she imagined royal princesses would have had when they were children. The bookshelf to the side was full of fantasy, and the teddy bears placed along it made her feel at home.

There was a fluffy white rug covering the floor space between the door and the foot of the bed, and a fresh set of pyjamas with slippers still with their labels on to welcome her in.

How lovely these people must be, she thought, and though the circumstances of their visit were dire, she felt as happy as she could be, still very excited for their dinner. Her dad was never long getting sorted and didn't mind living out of a bag, so he was quick to come and see if she was ready, and they headed down the winding staircase into the dining room.

'Blimey, that was quick!' Derek recalled looking up from his newspaper, genuinely shocked. 'This is Sandra.'

'So pleased to meet you, I've heard a lot about you,' Séan said with his friendly smile, taking her hand to kiss it. 'I'm Séan and this is my daughter Mary. We are so grateful to you two for putting us up for the time being'

'Pleasure. It's good to meet you too.'

From her looks, dress and accent, Mary had no doubt that Sandra was English. She was elegant in every move, and her style was so naturally pretty that every gesture she made just emphasised her beauty. She had one of those faces that was constantly smiling, even when she wasn't expressing any emotion at all. In fact, even if she was sad about something, Mary thought she would probably find something to smile about.

Despite all the niceties, Mary couldn't help but sense some hostility or uneasiness between Derek and Séan. She couldn't put her finger on exactly the vibe that she was getting, but from the conversations she had heard, there was something that didn't feel quite right. Overanalysing was an aspect of her personality which drove her mad, however, so she did try to stop thinking too deeply about it and thought instead perhaps the awkwardness was purely down to them having not seen one another for so long.

They sat down for their meal, and Mary was overly conscious of acting a certain correct way. She had never had to worry about etiquette before as most socialising was done among her wild family, so common courtesies were forgotten about, however on this occasion, she was only polite. 'Please' and 'thank you' were second nature phrases to her, but she also focussed on how she held herself and kept a constant thankful smile on her face for the kindness that these strangers were showing her.

Sandra brought out the main which was as English as you could get—bangers and mash. Mary loved this meal but had never seen a version presented as sophisticated as this one was. The creamy mash held the sausages in place which was all covered in thick onion gravy. The room filled with the fragrance of gravy which reminded her of being at McDintons on a Sunday among the delicious smelling roast dinners cooked by her mum. It was a perfect meal to have, and she was in no way putting on her delight. Dessert was even better, and she wondered if the O'Sullivan's had planned the meal entirely around her needs. Regardless, chocolate fudge cake was one of her favourites, and she indulged happily while her dad caught up with friends.

Despite feeling very tired, she managed to pay full attention to everything that was being said in order to find out details as to how her dad knew such rich and wonderful people. They spoke of fishing and holidays, other mutual friends and work. They spoke of her mother and some members of the family, but she sensed that Derek never knew the family overly well. It was that or there had been some upset between them in the past because there was still a slight uncomfortable feel that remained during the conversation, though it was less than before.

Maybe he moved to England years ago, so had simply lost touch with what he once knew. Her mind continued to play out different scenarios, and eventually she concluded that they worked together, fished together and went on one or two holidays, but this was before Derek had met Sandra, and they had almost entirely lost touch since until now.

Having remained at the table mostly staying focussed on the conversation between Sandra, Derek and her dad, Mary felt that slipping off to bed early wouldn't be frowned upon, particularly as she had had a busy day. She hugged them all but gave a tighter squeeze to her dad and ascended the stunning staircase to her temporary bedroom. It had always been a custom throughout her upbringing so far to give hugs generously, and she was taught to hug everybody that she knew. This resulted in her being a very tactile individual with a lot of love to share.

Once she reached the fluffy rug she decided against the new pyjamas because the ones she had brought smelt of home, and she wasn't ready to let go of that just yet. She did gladly accept the gift of the comfy slippers and put them on to go to the bathroom and brush her teeth before bed. This part of the day always made her feel independent because so often had she had to put herself to bed from a young age. No bitterness was held towards this on her part because it usually meant that her parents were having a good time, or it was when her mum had lost the ability and strength to function so she couldn't hold that against her.

She looked in the mirror while brushing her teeth and felt sadness for the loss of her mum. She felt gladness for the current situation she found herself in, and she felt fear for what the future would be like. She went back into her room and got her diary out of her bag for comfort. Keeping a short snippet of each day noted down was routine for Mary, but sometimes she felt compelled to write a letter too. Today was one of those days so she began writing.

Dear Brannagh,

Chapter 7
York, 1996

Mary paused for a moment during the process of getting ready for the ball to contemplate the fact that this was the end. The end of her fabulous time at university. The end of living with a brilliant group of girls who she desperately hoped not to ever lose touch with. They had made her feel more welcome in England than she had ever felt and were probably the first proper friendships she had made since living in the country.

The ball marked the end of independence as she would have to go back to living in London with her dad as neither her nor James could afford to buy or rent a house together until they both had decent jobs. Besides, Mary still had another year of education to go through before she would start earning a good salary because she wanted to become a teacher and had to do her PGCE year first. James hadn't decided on a career path and was going to do some labouring for his dad over the summer while he thought about the future which meant he would move back home to Suffolk.

All of this thinking about the end made Mary very sad. She was never good at goodbyes, and though none of them were going to be forever, she still found it hard to think about. At least she had the ball during which she planned to get rip roaring drunk and forget the end for now. After all, she wasn't moving back to London for another week and then had a girls' holiday as well as a weekend away in Bath with James to look forward to over the summer, which confirmed that all the goodbyes were only temporary.

Mary always needed evidence to back up her emotions in life. She couldn't simply accept that she would remain in touch with friends she had met at university and that her thoughts about James going off her once he moved back home were ridiculous, she needed plans to assure herself that things would happen the way she wished. Once the plans happened, she knew she would need to quickly make new plans for the not too distant future for her mind to settle again. She was okay with this and knew it was just how she was, she could never change it.

She looked in the mirror at her pale make-up free face and began to cry. She often cried when alone and was ironically happy to do so for nobody could witness her tears. Crying in front of people was a different thing altogether, and she could only recall two times that it had happened in her lifetime. Even when her dad told her the news of her mother's passing, she ran to her room to disguise her upset.

She was sat cross legged on the floor with one towel around her body and one wrapped neatly on the top of her head when she heard James call up the stairs which urged her to quickly wipe away the tears and continue getting ready.

'Come up!' she shouted down to him with happiness in her voice.

No matter what mood she was in, she could never hide the excitement of hearing the echo of low tones in his speech, knowing how much she loved his company. They had been together officially for two years and their relationship, though with its ups and downs, was one which everybody in the university was jealous of.

Everybody knew them or of them at least. The best thing about their relationship, forgetting all about the fame of it, was that what people perceived was very real. There was no glamour on the outside but difficulties lying underneath; it was a genuinely good bond that they shared together. Mary was so happy that she had waited for James to come along and that her first relationship was with him because they were both so relaxed, and there was no pressure on either side. Going with the flow was how they worked, and it worked really well.

'I would have put money on you being nowhere near ready,' James commented squeezing Mary's neck and giving her a kiss on the lips.

'Oh, shut up and fill up my glass.'

In true Mary fashion, she had already consumed over half a bottle of white wine prioritising her drunkenness over her looks. She was quite happy with the dress she had bought which was a silky navy blue fitted dress from Zara. It fell just above her knees, and she felt rather sophisticated in it because it cost her more money than she could afford. Jas had helped pick it out on one of their Saturday morning shopping trips which often turned out to be an all-day session because they would have multiple pub breaks and fall in the door at about 11.30 pm penniless and drunk.

There wasn't much rush for Mary to be ready in time because they were having everybody round to their house for drinks before they went to the ball, so she could afford to be running a little late. Jas and Michael were already drinking in the kitchen, so they could entertain any early arrivals. She only had her hair and makeup to do anyway which she was quicker at doing after a few glasses of wine, so she knew that she would be fine.

The doorbell rang, but luckily it was Sam, Lauren and Jules who seemed to be in high spirits due to the glorious sunshine and the bargain that they had just got for a crate of Carlsberg and four bottles of wine in Morrisons. Mary often laughed to herself when they came home after shopping trips, acting like three old women raving about the cheapness of a tin of beans. The guests, aside from boyfriends, were yet to arrive, leaving Mary more time to spend focussing closely on her eyeliner application due to a wobbly drunken hand.

James loved watching Mary get ready after she had had a few because she had a serious face on but would often make the funniest mistakes. One time she was putting liquid eyeliner on and spotted James smirking at her in the mirror which made her laugh and a large black streak of eyeliner ended up across her face.

'Careful doing that, it seems you've got the shakes,' James remarked, knowing that he would get a reaction from Mary.

'Funny one you are. Just let me concentrate and drink your drink, will you?' Mary replied.

By some miracle as was always the way during Mary's preparations for leaving the house, she managed to apply perfectly lined eye makeup which didn't show any signs of the amount of wine that had been consumed in the process.

'You look stunning,' James said with an amount of truth in his words but also knowing precisely what girls, particularly Mary, need to hear before a night out.

'Thank you, darling,' Mary replied in her sarcastic but appreciative tone. 'Shall we finish this bottle before joining the rest?'

A special thing about James and Mary's relationship was how much they loved spending time on their own. Mary's dad often said that for young people that was quite rare and that they should be out socialising more, but Mary and James loved both. They loved socialising and were always the last to leave parties or the club, but they also loved time to themselves just chatting and laughing over a bottle of wine, or occasionally no drink at all.

It never took them long to finish this amount of alcohol though, so soon enough they headed down to begin the celebrations with everybody else. The atmosphere in the house was always great, but Mary had the ability to make a bright room lighter simply by entering it. The music was already playing when Mary and James got to the kitchen, but Mary immediately turned up the volume and danced her way to the fridge to fill up everyone's glasses with the champagne that her dad had given her.

'Hey, Sam, what's that in your glass?' Mary asked judgingly. 'It's beer, why?' Sam replied confused at Mary's question.

'Tip it out, love. Tonight girl, we are on the Champagne, darling.'

To which Sam smiled and suddenly had more energy than before. That was another plus to Mary's character. She brought energy into the room, a kind which was hard to explain. Jas, Mary's best friend, had come to university a shy, self-conscious and rather sad young lady, but in Mary's presence, she instantly forgot about her past and gained a positive energy even if Mary wasn't saying or doing anything. It's why everybody loved to be around her. It was incredible.

The majority of people were out in the small concreted courtyard style garden, and more guests were entering through the side gate, so each time that Mary brought out glasses full of bubbly, she had to go back inside for more. Luckily, her dad was very generous and had provided six bottles of the good stuff for them all to enjoy. He had said he had to make the most of his only child graduating from university. A comment which caused a false smile, Mary knowing strongly that she wasn't his only child.

Number three, Lowther Crescent, where Mary and the girls lived, was always the first stop on nights out, and people throughout the university referred to it as the *party pad* because anyone who was anyone had been to one of their drinks gatherings. The mood of these parties was always so relaxed and happy putting everybody in fantastic spirits for the rest of the night.

Even though Jas had provided the sound system with her new stereo that she'd been given as an early graduation present from her parents, Mary always had the choice of CD because everybody loved her music taste. On this particular night, well, for this particular moment, she had chosen *Oasis* creating a chilled tone but still somewhat upbeat.

They all swayed along to the slower ones and sang their hearts out as soon as *Rock 'n' Roll Star* came blasting out of the speakers, which was when Jas turned up the volume and started throwing herself about. Fortunately, the girls had created a good rapport with their neighbours on both sides who weren't students, so they were let off at weekends when their place made a racket. In fact, occasionally the younger couple living to their left came over and joined in.

The taxis were booked, leaving everybody an hour to get merry before heading to the racecourse which was the glamorous venue for the ball. Some of the lads decided to walk despite it being about a forty-five-minute journey on foot, but they wanted to prove their manliness. All of the girls, however, went by car.

By the time that the taxis arrived, there wasn't a single sober person present, and Mary smiled at this having felt that she had hosted well. She and Jas were the last to leave the house, and while Jas was being sensible in doing the rounds to ensure everything was locked up, Mary was staring at the mess on the kitchen side and thinking how bad she would feel the next morning while extremely hungover and tidying it all away.

The group arrived in bulk and fashionably late, every girl remarking how beautiful every other girl looked and the guys heading straight to the bar. All in all, the vibes were just perfect, and Mary thought to herself how good a send-off the night was going to be. Jas had brought her top-quality camera to keep a record of it all, and she was the best person for this as she always forced everybody to have numerous photos in all sorts of poses, not caring how irritating she could come across.

Mary laughed as she accepted a glass of fizz from James and pointed out Jas mingling among the crowds and taking photos of people that none of them knew.

'We'll be her next victims,' James said with honesty as he hated having his photo taken.

He especially hated Jas being the instigator of his picture being taken as she wouldn't accept just the one, and the shoot would last for at least half an hour. When he noticed that Jas had seen the two of them and got a glimpse over Mary's shoulder of the rest of the group gathered at the other side of the room, they both dashed for them to avoid being held hostage by Jas and her Canon EOS 55.

Mary was the perfect personality to have during the awkward first stages of a formal event because she brought any group of people into fits of laughter. The part of the evening when everyone looked sophisticated, but nobody was having too much fun yet. The only time when groups of people who didn't really know or like each other would act interested in one another's lives. It was times like these when Mary's lively personality shone through and stood out like a planet among the twinkling stars in a clear night sky. This was one of the top things that James admired about her because he always remained quite reserved in big groups and only came out of his shell once he had had a few drinks, but socialising came so naturally to Mary.

What James was unaware of was that Mary had only come out of herself more through being in a relationship with him. The roles were reversed when they first met, and Mary's self-consciousness won, but after a strong two-year relationship with James her confidence had grown immensely, and she was the sociable one all of a sudden. She had always been funny but only truly to those close to her who she revealed her real self to. It used to take a while for her to show that side, but recently it gleamed openly and instantly to everyone she met.

The drinks continued to flow, and everyone was making top use of the free bar when everything fell silent for the awards. Mary had hoped that they wouldn't be serious ones like in school. Most improved academic, the award for history or sports captain. She hoped they would be lighter hearted which would give her a greater chance of winning something.

Most clumsy on a night out. Last to be ready and never on time. Biggest female drinker. Things like that would have Mary's name written all over them.

She soon discovered from the first award that it was a serious affair at York University, so she wished away that half an hour so that she could swiftly get onto the dance floor and drag everyone with her whether they wanted to dance or not.

'So without further ado, myself and the staff of the university would like to thank you class of 1996 for bringing us much joy and being a pleasure to teach. We wish you all every success in the future and a good night tonight. See you all at graduation, you've earned it.'

Finally, Mary thought, the old man had stopped blabbering on. Everything he was saying seemed scripted and something that would be heard at every university ball across the country.

She hoped that the graduation ceremony speeches wouldn't be as dire and unoriginal, but she expected that they would.

None of the speeches stayed with Mary from that night, but the night itself did as she knew it would. It was a formal summary of her time at university. It summarised the true friendships she had made, such as those who were willing to hold her hair back over the toilet while she regurgitated the shots she had just consumed. It outlined the fun that they had most nights during their time in York and how every one of them loved to have a good time and a laugh. The night demonstrated just how many friends she had made and how fabulous they all were with the ability to look amazing as well.

The final moments of the night while all sat out on the balcony at the venue looking up at the stars was one that should have been out of a film. It was a moment that was too good to be true, and though Mary had lost track of James' whereabouts, she was surrounded by great friends in one massive human hug.

What a perfect way to end a perfect chapter of her life, Mary considered, while pouring the dregs of empty bottles down the sink the following morning, severely hungover and feeling very sorry for herself.

Chapter 8
Dublin, 2018

I find myself in a scenario that I never expected during this stay. Sat at my laptop at eight o'clock in the morning and booking extra accommodation to extend our holiday. I suppose you could still call it that though it's beginning to feel like a chore, and after today, I think I will have forgotten about the relaxing aspect to the trip.

My mind keeps casting itself back to the sight I saw on the steps on Friday. The bruises as blue as you get and the swollen eye. I expected things to be bad but not quite this bad, and I can tell from my not being able to forget that image that I will be needed for a lot longer than a few hours on a Sunday afternoon. Why didn't I consider this, I muse, why was I so naïve?

I am very nervous about the meet up because we've still never actually met, though I feel that I know Brannagh having kept in constant contact over the years. I think there lies the problem because we talk so frequently and have become so involved with each other that I often forget the major issue that is scaring me the most—we have never met. I guess, we have a twenty first century bond though most of the bond was created via letters, so perhaps we were just ahead of the times, predicting the future virtual world and ability to have virtual relationships too.

I think back to all the letters I wrote her as a little girl. I wonder why I chose her to turn to rather than my own dad, my aunt or even friends. She was practically a stranger, but I was desperate to lean on her, and she has leant on me. That is just how it has worked forever, and we've never needed each other in reality because we always knew that we were virtually there. That has always been comforting enough through everything. Well, it has been for me anyway.

From the start of it all with Mammy's death to James' accident, I have always depended on her but never in person. It's not until she's reached out to me that I've realised how bizarre our bond and relationship could seem to others. The kids don't know anything about her which is why Daddy has kindly offered to take them off my hands today. I am yet to tell him about the time extension though.

I read over the most recent texts, the lengthier ones making me cry at her sheer desperation in such an awful situation. The time scale was something I continuously questioned before this trip, but what are you supposed to do when you have two young children in tow? I should have left them home with Daddy, but I needed them here for my own head.

I stop questioning my actions and get back into the zone of my online booking form with Booking.com. The ladies at reception, though attempting to be helpful, had no vacancies, so staying put in our flat is out of the question which is why I am hunting for similarly priced and central B&Bs before the children wake up. I realise that booking at such short notice is going to go against me, and I hope that this isn't a sign of how the rest of the day will pan out.

Erin sleepily enters the living space and squeezes up to me on the sofa as I quickly shut the laptop and place it on the table to the side. She gives me a gentle cuddle which is exactly what I need, and without having to tell her about my struggles and fears for today, she seems to know something is unsettling me and comforts me perfectly.

'Thank you, darling. Did you sleep okay?' I ask, and she looks at me unsure as to why her hugging her mum required a 'thank you'.

'Yes. When is Granddad arriving?'

'He should be leaving for the airport in about an hour. He'll be with us by midday. Would you like a drink?'

'Orange juice please.' It's mornings when Erin is at her best. She shows all the signs of love and affection that have always been there but have seemed to vanish recently behind the frustration and anger towards the world that comes with being fourteen years old.

I push the laptop further away realising that this precious time in Erin's golden hour is more important and get up to make us both a drink. I've already had a cup of tea, but Mammy always said that no day should begin with less than two cups. It was one of her better pieces of advice, so I think of her and put the kettle on. I smile to myself while looking out of the window and forgetting all worries when my phone begins to buzz in my pocket.

I see the word *Daddy* and instantly feel the bad news that is about to hit me. I don't know why I don't consider that it may be him just letting us know he's leaving or perhaps he has arrived at the airport early, but I instantly think it'll be bad. I want to cry when he tells me that he has to stay home on doctor's orders. I hardly listen to his medical reel off about what is wrong with him, and I am shocked at my reaction not realising how much I needed him here. Not only for the children but as a support for me. He doesn't know the full story, but I was going to tell him everything as soon as he arrived. I need to tell him everything. I need him.

As ever he is one step ahead and supportive from afar having arranged for Aunt Eileen to come and meet us to take care of the children, but I had no intentions of telling anybody else the situation apart from Daddy. Aunt Eileen is Daddy's eldest sister, and she has a whacky but warm and comforting aura about her. She won't understand immediately and will probably attempt to persuade me not to get involved, but when she can see how much I care then she will come around for sure. My instant reaction when he tells me is to panic at a stressful situation being changed and unsettled more, but once I have thought about it for a few minutes, I feel much calmer.

'Okay, darling. Now are you going to tell me what this is all about?' Daddy asks, suggesting that he knows that I am up to something.

'What?' I reply acting dumb.

'Look, Mary. I know you, and I know this trip wasn't just a spur of the moment revisit to your roots.'

So, I tell him—everything—wondering how a man can be so wise to my every move and read through me so thoroughly and accurately. It's difficult to properly explain with Erin sat in the next room, so I am careful to be quiet so that she doesn't cotton on.

At first, he is shocked and claims that he didn't suspect a thing. He told me of times when he'd notice me writing letters as a child, and he assumed that they were to Mammy. She's dead, I'm not that strange, I think, but then I suppose that is how some young girls would cope. I do feel quite comforted that he had the decency to keep my privacy private despite being a lone parent of a young girl. I imagine how I would react if it was me with Erin which makes me admire his care more. He said he felt warmed that this was how I had chosen to handle things, but he didn't hide the fact that he was afraid of me meeting her and getting involved with the issues she is facing.

A few minutes of good conversation with my dad swayed him to stick with me and support me through it knowing that his sister would be one of the best people I could have by my side and would have a solution to any struggle I face over the course of the next week.

As I have done so many times before, I quickly wipe my face free of tears and get back to my cup of tea and Erin's juice. I walk back into the living room and feel proud to see my daughter taking in the streets below, no electronic devices in sight. In silence having still not figured how to work the television, we enjoy our morning beverages before getting dressed for the day.

While searching for my new mascara to complete my look for the day, I hear a knock at the door and notice that time has flown, and it is just before eleven o'clock. Eileen comes in, and after the usual delighted greetings between the two of us and more awkward cuddles with the children, we attempt to work out when we last saw each other.

My aunt has always been good to me. She keeps in regular contact, and if it isn't a phone call to me then she will ring Daddy and ask about us every week. She used to visit us in London all the time and came to see me at uni a few times as well as staying with us for a fortnight in York every summer. Her visits lately have been scarcer due to life getting in the way and her ageing body finding the trip that bit more tiring, but we predict it has been about a year since we have seen each other in person.

It is so refreshing to have adult company with me, and I decide to forget the circumstances and just enjoy the next hour with my wonderful aunt. We decide to go for an early lunch in the city which is when I wish I hadn't given up the drink because an ice-cold beer or vodka on the rocks would go down beautifully now and calm some of my nerves which are building up fast.

We head out to the closest pizzeria for ease and to get ourselves more time together to attempt to subtly discuss my intentions without the children hearing a word. We find one with outside seating which is perfect because after the meal Erin happily takes Jack away to play on the play equipment, giving me and Eileen a chance to catch up.

Erin always reverts to her childlike ways when Eileen is around, and I haven't ever known why but I love it. Eileen has the power to keep her great niece young, innocent and nice to be around which is rare at the moment, not to sound awful. I also love Eileen because her honesty is reliable, and I can count on her to tell me exactly what she thinks and whether she thinks I am doing the right thing.

'Do you think I'm being bonkers Auntie? I just don't know another solution,' I ask as if she's my mother.

I suppose she has taken place as my motherly figure when I have needed advice without me knowing. She is the lady I would always turn to if the advice I required was specifically female. Daddy was my go-to for everything, but there were certain things that he couldn't answer and certain words of wisdom I needed to hear from a woman.

'I don't think you're nuts, darling. I think you're incredibly brave.'

Hearing these words from someone so special to me gives me the strength to want to go ahead with my plans again, and I stop questioning my actions altogether knowing that to me it was the morally correct thing to do.

I look at my phone to see that half an hour has passed when Erin and Jack return to us with their happy faces on. I think to myself how perfect the day is working out even squeezing in a good chat with Eileen away from the children. It's as if somebody is watching over me and moving the timings around so that things work in my favour. Like a giant human being playing a game of chess with us all. It's Mammy, I think and smile with my children wishing that the day from hell won't be so hellish after all.

Eileen has planned a river cruise for the children this afternoon giving me plenty of time to freshen up, meet Brannagh and compose myself afterwards depending on how it goes. Also, them being on the river gives me a good sense of their whereabouts so that we won't accidentally bump into each other. The children are asking enough questions already, and they don't need to know.

After a delicious Pepperoni pizza and a lunch on Eileen, I give all three of them huge hugs and we part, them heading to the river and myself back to the flat to put on my strong face and go to do some good.

As I turn from my family, a tear trickles down my face. A tear of worry but also sadness that I can't be with them enjoying a quality family afternoon together. I miss those times. I also think about Daddy and how little I listened to him on the phone, so I can't recall what he said was wrong with him. It can't be too bad else Eileen would have mentioned it. However, I was rather preoccupied dominating the conversation, so she may have wanted to mention it but instead kept it in for a later date. I am sure he will ring me again later, and I can ask him properly then. My stomach begins to feel sick.

I have spoken with Brannagh throughout my life, but virtual bonds are very different to reality. Especially, a reality as harsh as this one, and I have no idea what to expect when I see her. Though I have had her phone number for some years now we have only ever texted, never phoned. I have never heard her voice. I have never seen her in person until Friday afternoon. I can only imagine what she is going to be like. I begin to feel slightly guilty that she had to reach out to me, and I never thought of physically being there for her though I said in a lot of my messages that I was. I am there, I want to be there, but I wish the scenario was more pleasant.

I arrive back at the flat with a good hour to spare before having to leave to meet her, so I decide a nice cup of tea will make things a bit clearer. I think of Mammy's reliance on cups of tea and try to relax in the comfort of this memory. I sit on the edge of the sofa clenching my mug and staring out of the window onto the busy street. I remember yesterday morning when I was in the exact same scene but with my young daughter clinging onto me and how I felt much more comfortable then. I think of just a few hours prior when Erin and I were in the exact same setting.

I snap out of my ridged frame and lean back into the sofa, sinking into the cushion to hold me and take another gulp of my tea. The relaxing feeling seems to give me strength and for a snippet I feel all right about what is to come. A text comes through from Brannagh confirming the time and place, and instantly all of my nerves reappear.

We have decided to meet at a bar which I guess is so that she can have a drink to make her feel better while delivering the awful story. Little does she know that I no longer have this privilege, though I have made it that way through choice. Maybe I could have one little drink. I consider whether I feel strong enough to cope but soon come to the conclusion that this scenario is not the right one to make that bold move. It needs to be done in a happier, calmer environment and mindset. I praise myself for my own sensibility and leave.

Walking along the streets brings me a huge sense of being home. Especially, having spent some time with Eileen and a phone call with Daddy, I feel as though I have gone back in time thirty years or more. Part of me begins to wish I could and fix the relationship that I have formed with Brannagh into a real one rather than virtual. My mind goes crazy with thoughts of what could have been. I contemplate how different my life could have turned out. Then I forget my regrets and continue to walk.

I get my trusty map out and again think how bizarre it is that my sense of direction of this place has vanished. Granted place names change in thirty years, so I can forgive myself for not recognising the name of the bar, but the streets seem alien to me, the same streets I walked up and down for the first decade of my life. I contemplate taking a detour to the spot where McDintons used to be and wonder what it has been replaced with. Perhaps it is still there. Though time is pressing on, so I decide to leave that to after our meet. Besides, I would probably end up lost judging by my directional skills so far.

Eventually, I reach the bar and spot that same face that I saw only the other day, but now it's looking cleaner and has an expression of forced joy rather than being totally expressionless. I predict it's forced due to my knowledge of the situation we are about to discuss, but then note that I have never known her person, so perhaps that is just how she smiles. I am glad we instantly recognise each other withdrawing my first fear having only ever seen pictures which could be so different from reality.

'This is so surreal,' she says to me before saying anything else, and I immediately go back to the first time I met James when my ability to converse temporarily vanished. Thankfully, I have grown a lot since then and swiftly manage to confidently continue the conversation.

'This is my shout, you grab a table, and I will get the drinks in.'

While waiting to be served, I revise what just happened and think how differently it went to how I expected. I hate situations like this because I can't help but evaluate my every action and all the words that I say. Luckily, not many left my mouth though I do feel quite rude and that I should have given her a hug or something more normal. However, I realise that we both feel quite strange, so it went well considering.

Chapter 9
London, 1988

They had certainly timed this trip well, Mary thought while putting on her new shoes for her first day at the school. They had been in England for three weeks, and she hadn't had to worry about making new friends or whether the girls were going to be nasty, nor even if they would be able to understand her accent because she had been blissfully unaware of all those nerves during her stay at the palace. Derek and Sandra had treated her like a princess, and they had been on lots of exciting days out, her favourite being the one that they spent visiting Buckingham Palace followed by a boat trip on the Thames.

If she was honest with herself, then a day spent helping Derek in the garden or baking with Sandra was enjoyable enough as they were lovely people and the closest experience that Mary had of a proper functioning parental unit for a long while.

Séan was handling the move surprisingly well considering the fact that he hated change, but then Mary soon acknowledged that he had chosen it this time, so he couldn't exactly be down about things. Especially, as for the first time since all that had happened, he seemed to be truly content, living a good life with old friends and his daughter in a country full of new opportunities. Everything was upbeat, and they already had some wonderful memories of England.

What wasn't so wonderful, however, was how Mary was feeling about starting a new school. She paid a visit to Chiswick School a week before the start of term in her father's attempt to reassure her that a new school wasn't going to be so bad and to familiarise herself with the building so it wouldn't feel completely alien on the day.

The building was huge and looked much like a hospital which it probably used to be, Mary assumed, and she felt that she would never be familiar with any part of it despite her dad's best efforts. The memory sat embedded in her mind of the rigid structure and huge amount of prison like windows, yet for some reason it was still so dark inside. There was a significant lack of greenery around the grounds to add to this institutional feel, and it didn't add any warmth to the place that she would spend a large chunk of her teenage years inside either.

Not only did the building frighten her, Mary was also scared about the fact that she would be starting in year ten. She felt that it was an awkward time to move schools because everybody else would be settled in with their own friendship groups that she would have to somehow fit in to. It would be as if school social circles were a jigsaw puzzle, but she was the random piece that had got mixed up with a separate jigsaw. She knew that her dad was trying to make it as easy for her as possible, but it didn't take away the fact that she was terrified.

All the fear inside Mary made her gladder that Sandra was taking her in on her first day. Her dad had felt bad that he couldn't be there to support her, but he was starting his new job as a manager at a restaurant down the road and needed to make a good first impression, so Sandra had kindly stepped in. It was big new starts for them both, a lot of firsts and a lot of new experiences.

Over the past few weeks, Mary and Sandra had developed a relationship from complete strangers to a bond like that shared between a mother and daughter which was exactly what Mary needed in the current difficult times. Though she hardly spoke about her feelings and usually turned to her diary to let out her angst, on the occasion that she needed to talk to somebody, Sandra was always available and gave good hugs as well as effective advice. She knew that she could confide in her dad, but he was finding things tricky, and often she wanted somebody completely separate from the family so that they wouldn't have already formed opinions on matters. Impartiality was precisely what she needed, and Sandra was conscious of keeping her views impartial, having never met, let alone heard about those who Mary spoke of.

Mary rarely opened her heart to anybody about the family situation or anything else for that matter, but she did desperately want to speak openly about her fears of starting a new school. Sandra must have sensed this when she came up the stairs with a mug of juice and some toast for Mary as Mary finished tying her right shoelace.

'Everything okay, poppet?' Sandra asked genuinely caring about how Mary was feeling about the big day.

'I am a bit nervous, but I think I have everything so I'm ready. I think.'

'Take your time. Here, sit on your bed and enjoy your breakfast. I'll sit with you if you want to talk?' Sandra directed these words as a question to which Mary just smiled awkwardly, and Sandra knew she simply wanted her to be there; not necessarily to be saying anything, just to remain beside her.

It was incredible how Sandra and Mary had built such a close bond in such a short amount of time. The intenseness of their relationship had meant that they had got to know each other extremely fast, and Sandra had taken Mary under her wing. It provided something for them both; Mary needed a female motherly figure to lean on, finding life harder than she had anticipated without her own mother, and Sandra had always wanted children but sadly couldn't have them. She was showing her ability of being a good mum which she knew she already had in her, and it seemed to come naturally. Séan frequently thanked her for this.

Derek had also been a perfect friend to Séan, and Mary soon came to realise why he had chosen to come and stay with this couple of all the places he could have chosen. However, confusion remained over why they hadn't been in touch for so long.

None of these random thoughts were going to help Mary through her first day at a big scary school so she soon tucked them away for later. Instead, she began to quiz Sandra about what the school would be like. She had no idea that Sandra didn't attend Chiswick School and knew so little about it that she needed to use a map to get there.

'What if all of the girls hate me?' Mary asked Sandra followed by a sweet chuckle immediately realising how presumptuous she was being and a little over the top.

'They would be fools to hate you.' Sandra replied, always using the most comforting phrases.

For a moment, Mary felt quite okay and even confident about going, but as soon as they approached Sandra's red Volvo, her nerves returned. Sandra was a few minutes inside shutting the dogs away while Mary waited anxiously in the car. She looked over the leaflet that she had been given by the head teacher on her visiting day and glared at the size of the building. Schools were definitely smaller in Ireland, or perhaps just felt smaller because she was familiar with them.

They set off out of the grand gates and on with their journey which was to become part of their daily routine. Mary took in all her surroundings in an attempt to forget about her worry. Luckily the sun was shining, and London was looking bright which helped lift her mood up slightly. She could see groups of children dressed in uniforms very different to hers, laughing as they walked to their various schools. She spotted a few people in her uniform, and they looked quite normal in her opinion, so she wondered if they would be in her year group. Maybe they would become friends and in a few weeks' time she too would be walking to school with them.

She then wondered why Sandra was driving if the school was a walking distance away from the house. Yet from Sandra's well-disguised frustration so not to panic Mary more, it was quite clear that she hadn't had a clue where she was going.

Finally, they reached the school car park, and Mary was positive that they had gone around in circles a few times on their way, but Sandra had been too kind to Mary for her to begin nit-picking at her navigational skills. The car park was as busy as Mary had imagined it would be, crammed full of cars and students with the odd teacher trying to shepherd everybody in, in an orderly fashion, but failing.

The blank expressions on Sandra and Mary's faces were clearly evident as a lady approached them asking if they were new to the school too. The lady's daughter, who was stood shyly behind her, was starting year nine having moved up from Dorset.

'This is Evelyn. She is very nervous,' said the mother with an annoyance about her that Mary couldn't help but get irritated with.

'Hi,' she replied bluntly, and they all sensed that the encounter would go no further, heading off in opposite directions.

Mary was becoming more and more overwhelmed as swarms of children came flooding into the huge building. She had no idea how she was going to make any friends. It was as if there were so many people that she wouldn't know where to begin with her greetings and introductory conversation. She even doubted she would be able to find her classroom or who to speak with to get any sense of the place. This was when she became so grateful again for Sandra's presence, taking it upon herself to find the headmaster's office and settle Mary's nerves before she did anything else.

'Welcome to Chiswick High School, Mary. How are you today?' The gentleman spoke with an exaggerated version of the posh accents that Mary had first witnessed at the airport, and she tried very hard not to smirk.

'I'm good. A little nervous,' she replied sounding more confident than she felt.

'Well, you have got nothing to worry about. We will look after you. You'll now spend the next twenty minutes with me going through a few things, and then I will hand you over to Miss Richardson who will take care of you throughout your first day.'

Mr Smith's authoritative tone had given Mary the confidence to let Sandra leave, a decision she immediately regretted as soon as the door closed behind her.

As Mr Smith showed Mary around the school, she felt thankful, looking into classrooms of hard-working students, that she was getting out of the first lesson or two, but this didn't remove any of her fears. The classes looked more serious than they had been back home, but then she thought that might be down to the fact that she had all her friends with her to laugh and joke with.

The girls in classes that Mr Smith went in and introduced Mary to had seemed to be giving her stern looks, but she wasn't sure if this was in her imagination or not. Regardless, she had better get used to it because she figured that these classes were the ones she would be going to.

After a twenty-minute tour that felt a lot longer and some introductory papers that Mary had been through with Miss Richardson, it was time for her first class which was going to be music.

She had never heard of GCSEs back in Ireland and soon realised they had only recently been introduced to England. She made this judgement from the confusion faced when she chose her options with the lady who had first shown her around the school when her and her dad first visited a week ago. She hadn't taken her choices overly seriously because it had all been too much for her, and she was still in the mix of getting used to her new life. Besides she hadn't got a clue what she wanted to be when she grew up so didn't think that these choices mattered too much. One thing she did know was that she loved to teach so perhaps that would be an option, but you can teach any subject, so again she felt that the choices weren't as important to her as all the adults around her were making out at the time.

One thing she did love was music, so this being her first lesson to trial her new school brought her some happiness. From a young age she had been encouraged to learn an instrument and was grateful that her mum had chosen to get her piano lessons on her eighth birthday. Through all the chaos of the past few years she had given up lessons, but she had built up a talent and would often tinkle away on the keys if ever she was close by one.

Miss Richardson was her guide for the week, collecting her and dropping her at each lesson so she would never get lost. Mary's music class was held in room seventeen where Miss Richardson left her, and she stood outside in anticipation for whatever came next. Mary was only five minutes early so a small queue had already built up outside the door waiting for the teacher to come along, and she stood about halfway up and began chatting to a pretty blonde girl while waiting.

'I'm new here. What's the teacher like?' She felt this was a good opener because they could joke about if the teacher was horrid.

'He's lovely. Music is my favourite subject. I'm Karen by the way. And you are?'

'Mary.'

Another advantage Mary had to starting new conversations was her accent. If ever the recipient of her chat couldn't think of another topic to discuss they always went for the accent option. Mary enjoyed this because not only was she very proud to be Irish, it opened up a lot of things to say, and the conversation would usually continue to flow without any awkward hesitation.

'So, you're Irish?' Karen said, immediately stating the obvious and removing Mary's initial judgement of her being a bright girl.

'Of course. Does my accent not give it away?' Mary asked trying extra hard not to be blunt or sarcastic and letting the statements that she would exchange with her dad after school remain for now inside her head.

'Where in Ireland are you from?'

'Dublin. Have you ever been?'

'No, never. My mother is from Northern Ireland, Belfast, I think. I'm unsure because we're not very close with that side of the family, and I've never been there.'

Instantly the conversation was going as Mary had expected once her accent revealed her roots, and she was glad to be so easily chatting to her new friend. Could she call Karen that already? They were in school, so she figured that she could.

Eventually, a lady who Mary assumed was the music teacher guided the long queue of students into the room and pulled Mary aside to have a quiet welcome chat with her. Mary wasn't really listening to what the lady was saying and couldn't even remember her introducing herself because she was more concerned about there being a spot next to her new friend Karen so that she wouldn't be alone during lesson number one.

'Other than that, just enjoy yourself. I hear music is your favourite subject?' The lady continued, and Mary reverted her attention to the conversation, desperately trying to work out what had been said.

'Yes, I love it.'

The long pause after her statement implied that their chat was over and Mary was free to sit down. Luckily, Karen had clearly enjoyed their first conversation while waiting for class and invited Mary to sit beside her.

The class was full of highly enthusiastic peers, and Mary already liked the atmosphere. She had been having nightmares about bullies and horrible judgemental girls which she realised had been a bit overcritical since she herself had never before set foot in England. Instead, she felt she was among lots of happy and pleasant people, though it had only been ten minutes. Optimism was always a good way forward.

The lady who Mary could not remember the name of was at the front of the class, setting up what looked like a load of African tribal instruments.

'Today's topic is African Music,' Karen said noticing Mary's look of confusion at the Lamellophone, Wood Claves and Shekeres sitting on the floor.

'Sounds like fun,' Mary replied. 'Is that our teacher?'

'No. Miss Dobson is just an assistant. Mr Charlesworth is always late, but he is lovely too.'

Mary was thankful that Karen was one step ahead and had answered her next, quite embarrassing question which would have been asking what Miss Dobson's name was.

Mr Charlesworth arrived apologising for his lateness, but swing band had ran over which pleased Mary because she had been part of a swing band in her old school and loved it. Every moment of being part of it was thoroughly enjoyable, and the best bit was that the audience loved it too. She knew instantly that she would be finding out the details on that after class as her musical involvement was something that she was never shy about.

The first lesson went a lot smoother than Mary had played out in her head so many times over the past week. She had made a few friends and was grateful for Karen who had been loyal so far. Miss Richardson met her as promised and led her to the next class, but Karen was with them the whole way, and Miss Richardson clocked this and seemed happy that Mary appeared to be settling in so quickly. Perhaps a new start wasn't going to be so scary after all.

Chapter 10
London, 1988

It had been three weeks since that dreaded first day of school, and Mary was settling in a lot better than she had expected to. Karen remained by her side, and the longer she spent with her newly established friend, the more she felt that not only had Karen been a blessing for Mary, but it was the other way around too.

Fully aware as to how presumptuous she was being, Mary had predicted that before she joined Chiswick High School, Karen had been quite the loner. The sort of girl who sat on the front row but never said a word, yet when spoken to she had everything needed to be sociable and accepted by society. Mary didn't understand why because she was lovely and didn't shy away from conversation as she had demonstrated on that first day when she approached Karen before music class. Perhaps she hadn't found the person who she clicked with and just needed to meet a friendly Irish girl to find that click.

It was a bright, sunny Friday, and Mary liked the look of her lesson plan for the day. Sometimes, usually for the less academic subjects, the school doubled up periods so that you got longer time spent on one lesson. This particular Friday her double lesson was music which pleased her immensely.

She was quite proud of herself to have grasped the timetable system so quickly because when Mr Smith went through everything on the introductory day she was left dazzled and confused. However, she realised that there was so much information to take in on that day, so she could let herself off a little.

Considering she had only had three weeks practice and despite having to check each morning so she knew whether to pack her sports kit or not, she felt she had cottoned on pretty quickly. The structure changed for alternate weeks so on the first week of term you would have week A and one set of lessons, then the following week you would have the same lessons but in a different order and a few extras added in. Then this would repeat until you eventually left, went to college or got a job.

Sandra dropped Mary at the usual place just a bit up the road from the entrance to the car park. They had decided on this plan early on because the car park got mad, and Mary liked that small piece of independence that she got each morning walking the hundred metres or so into school on her own. Occasionally, she would arrive at the same time as Karen, and they would head in together, but usually Karen was late, so Mary would go in alone.

Gradually, she was recognising more faces to smile at as she walked to her form class at the beginning of the day, and this made her happy. There was always the group of boys hanging around the lockers of which she only knew two by name, Luke and Josh, but they all always said hello.

Then as she headed further down the corridor, she would often see Miss Richardson chatting to the cleaner, and they too would both greet her jollily. That was one of the best traits that Miss Richardson possessed in Mary's opinion. The way that she was a higher member of staff to so many, yet she would always pay special attention to those at the bottom and treat them with as much respect as she would have towards those at the top. She continued to check on Mary weekly, but already Mary had settled in so well that her daily check-ups were not necessary.

Mary reached her tutor class and stood outside with Lucy and Erin, two girls who were always early and stood there waiting each morning when she arrived. They were nice enough to chat to, but she never spent time with them elsewhere. However, she always knew that if Karen was ever ill then she would have people to sit with during form class at least.

It was funny, she often thought, how many things you had to consider on top of education while at school. There were so many aspects to the social side of things that her mind felt like it was going to explode on numerous occasions simply by taking everything into account. Most things she hoped wouldn't follow her into adulthood, but she predicted that they may well do. Worrying about what people thought and always having a backup friend so she never looked like a loner. Acting a certain way in front of certain people so they thought she looked cool. Pretending to enjoy certain hobbies to fit in with the crowd. Social life was a minefield that Mary couldn't ever see herself getting the hang of.

She always thought herself quite lucky to have moved schools at such an awkward time under dire circumstances because she got pandered to a lot. They hadn't assigned her a form class before she came, and it wasn't until the end of day one when she was asked if there were any particular students that she felt she'd like to be in a tutor group with. Luckily, she had met Karen that day, so she was put into her tutor group. Though Karen was quite often late, so Mary would be sat on her own until she came in halfway through the register being called.

The register was another aspect to England that she felt was strange—that in England they still called out registers even when you were fourteen years old and at high school. Back at home, they gave up on that after primary school, and you would just sign yourself in on a sheet at the front of the class which felt much more grown up and efficient.

Tutor group was only twenty minutes, and the first lesson of the day was Mathematics, so Mary was glad to see Karen arrive in the final two minutes else she would have been too bored to cope. Maths was not a favourite subject for Mary, and the only thing that kept the two girls going through the lessons were the group of boys who sat on the back row and ridiculed the teacher, which everybody found hilarious. Everybody, except the teacher of course, but Mrs Gwenigault wasn't clever enough to overrule them, so just let them get on with it while attempting to teach trigonometry.

The Maths floor was right at the top of the building on one side, and the English floor was at the top but on the other side, so the students got their fair share of exercise merely getting from one lesson to the next. The staff who created the timetables tried not to put the two subjects consecutively or at least have break time in between because there was only a five-minute time period in which to get to the next lesson, and the corridors got rammed with pupils so you would never have made it in time. Not to mention the accidents that could occur on route due to a lack of staff on crowd control.

People would bash into one another, maybe even knock people to the floor. One poor boy got quite badly hurt from being trampled during the mad rush between lessons once; it was awful. The teachers tried their best to prevent such incidents, though there were always hiccups in systems like this, and of course, Mary's timetable contained one of these. Maths followed by English on a Monday morning, the worst.

While browsing her timetable each day Mary often wondered how long the creating of them took. It must be such a difficult task, like having a jigsaw, but all the pieces were painted black so you had no idea what the final image was supposed to be, nor could you work out how each piece fitted together from that image. She didn't know the answer, but she did know she never wanted that job.

The day was going smoothly, and having double music for her final two periods as well as knowing that she was making blackberry crumble with Sandra over the weekend made it a very happy Friday indeed. In music, the class were working on composing a short piece in a group using whatever musical instruments they could find within the music block which at Chiswick High School was huge. It was where Mary's piano abilities played to her advantage because she would be able to lead the group and fill out any empty sounds with her melodies that she could create, putting their end product above the rest of the class purely down to her talent. She had played for so long and built up a talent good enough that no amount of time away from a piano would ever remove it. As soon as she was sat at the black-and-white keys and put her fingers to them, she could come up with something; she wasn't shy about playing in front of people either. It came totally naturally to her.

'Cor you're really good at that,' said one member of their group who Mary hadn't yet learnt the name of while she was improvising and everybody else was choosing instruments to use.

'Thank you,' Mary replied modestly.

She never noticed her talent because she thoroughly enjoyed playing. It was her way of escaping, and sometimes she failed to hear the music coming from the tips of her fingers because she had left the world altogether. It was a great feeling, so she didn't much care what it sounded like to others.

The end of the school day came quicker than usual because Mary was having so much fun in her music class, and it was time to walk to her spot to meet Sandra in the red Volvo. Her mood was lifted even further because it was the weekend, and the four of them were off to the coast for a miniature get away. She hadn't been to the beach in England yet, and living so close to the sea throughout her childhood, she knew it would bring her a sense of home.

Sandra and Derek owned a caravan in a park on the coast right by the sea and used it often so were very excited to introduce Séan and Mary to their hideaway. Mary had got so excited the night before that she had packed her bags already, but Sandra mentioned another job she had to do before they set off. She had to help Derek pick the blackberries for the crumble that Sandra and she would make the following day. Mary grinned at this news because she loved time spent in the garden with Derek and all that they chatted about. Equally, she loved baking with Sandra, and it was the closest she felt she could get to her mum apart from speaking to her when nobody else was around, but she didn't mention that.

Derek was already outside enjoying the glorious Indian summer sunshine in September when he noticed Mary come trundling along with a cheerful bounce to her step.

'I've been waiting for you, darling,' he said with happiness in his voice.

Derek and Sandra hadn't any children of their own nor did they have any young children in their family, so they had both taken a strong liking to having Mary stay with them. Not only because they felt she was a lovely girl, but she also provided them with an opportunity to nurture that they had so much longed for.

'Are you excited to see the sea?' Derek asked Mary as she threw her school bag on the ground and started picking.

'Yes, so much.'

She couldn't hide the excitement if she tried and hoped that it would give her the homely feeling that she desired. Not only did the sea make her feel at home but it seemed to literally wash all the troubles that she had away. She frequently took herself to Sandymount and relaxed during her final year in Dublin. She wasn't really allowed to go there on her own, but with the turmoil going on in the family, nobody took much notice of her whereabouts, and she had a free reign. She would walk right up to the shoreline, look right out to sea and feel the weight she had been carrying lift off her shoulders. She didn't know where it went, but she was glad that it was away from her.

She discussed this sensation with Derek over their fruit picking, and he agreed. He was amazed at the adult conversation topics that came from Mary, and he enjoyed his time in the garden with her as he would if it were spent with an adult.

'You received a letter in the post today,' he remarked at random.

'Oh, did I?' Mary pondered, questioning who would be writing to her and why they hadn't addressed it to her and her dad as it would only be from family.

'Yes. Let's fill this bucket and then I will go and get it for you.'

They were picking the last of the blackberries, and Mary was wondering how many crumbles they were making from the number of buckets they had filled. Then Derek informed her that they would dish them out to their neighbours to Mary's relief. Although she loved baking with Sandra, she felt one crumble was enough.

For the last half a bucket of blackberries they picked, Mary had gone quieter racking her brain as to who the letter could be from. She never received mail addressed only to her, it was always addressed to both her and her dad, and it was usually Aunt Eileen. She hurried to fill the bucket so that she could get hold of the letter and work out from the handwriting who it was from.

Derek took two buckets, and Mary took the other plus the tools that they had out beside them into the house. Sandra and Séan were loading the car when Derek passed the letter to Mary. At a first glance she didn't recognise the handwriting and felt strongly that she had never received a letter from the sender before. She ran up the winding stairs to grab her bag and investigate.

She couldn't open the letter quickly enough noting how little time she would have alone because Sandra's timetable was tight, and Mary and Derek had already taken longer than intended in the garden. She placed her thumb in the corner and ripped open the envelope, not attempting to read a word, only the signature at the bottom. Brannagh. It was from Brannagh. Her first letter of many and one that she never thought would appear.

Mary was being called continuously from downstairs. They were urging her to hurry which made her forget to read the contents of the letter even though she desperately wanted to. She grabbed her bag and ran down the stairs as quickly as she had ran up them. She took a thin jacket which was hanging on the bannister and placed the letter carefully inside the pocket ensuring it stayed with her in the car and wasn't stored away in the boot with the rest of the baggage.

Everybody was waiting for Mary once she got downstairs and into the car, Sandra just had to lock up, load the dog into the boot and then they were off. She was still very excited about the prospect of the beach, yet Mary couldn't get the questions over the letter out of her head. She desperately wanted some privacy so that she could read it, but Sandra was sat across from her in the car and would quiz her if she got it out. She could probably pass it off as a love letter from somebody back in Dublin and Sandra wouldn't take it any further, but she didn't want to take the risk. Luckily Derek and Sandra's caravan had three bedrooms, so Mary would have space and time then to see what Brannagh's reply revealed.

The sea was an hour and a half drive away, and Derek and Séan had the football on the radio and shouted at Sandra and Mary for exchanging any amount of conversation like the typical men that they were. Not being able to win in a male dominated environment, the two girls both got out their books and read. Mary didn't read a word and constantly thought how she could subtly place the letter inside her book to look as though she was reading the story but actually read the letter instead. However, her coat was by her feet, so anybody would notice her plan.

The traffic was surprisingly good throughout the journey which Derek claimed was down to his efficient planning and time scale. Yet Sandra argued that was her doing and he had never stuck to a timetable in his life, while Séan urged them to be quiet so he could listen to the football.

Regardless as to who was the planning guru, they arrived in daylight, and Mary stood out of the car on the grass beside the caravan and looked out at the sea. For a moment she forgot she was in England and felt firmly at home. For a moment she forgot all about the letter, simply breathed in the sea air and soaked up the moment of total relaxation. Peace at last, and she hadn't realised how much she had missed it.

Chapter 11
Dublin, 2018

I return to the table with a drink filling each hand and in a state of temporary shock at how much I just paid for them. Fair enough, I think to myself, Brannagh's gin and tonic would have been pretty costly anywhere you went. Her preference of the aromatic Fever Tree tonic adds to the expense, but I must keep her sweet on this occasion and inevitably let the niceties wear off as we go on becoming the sisters that we are. However, my choice of pink lemonade bringing the grand total at the bar to eighteen euros hasn't pleased me at all. Granted they have added a few raspberries for good measure, but it is certainly not worth that amount unless the raspberries have some kind of gem hidden within them. I hope to God that is the case, but I highly doubt that it is.

'Thank you,' my sister says with that familiar Irish accent, something that I have missed over the years having only heard my dad's on a regular basis and Aunt Eileen's, but she's sounding frailer now. It is refreshing to hear a young and new one.

As I sit and admire my glass of very expensive lemonade and contemplate what I am doing with my life because it hasn't even the hint of alcohol in it, I feel contentment in my bones at being in the company of my sister. Though I realise that this meeting isn't going to be full of good news, I take a moment to enjoy the fact that such an awful situation has finally brought us together, and while thinking of a conversation starter with somebody who is in desperate need, I smile inside at this feeling.

'You're most welcome. So, you've never moved away then?' I ask Brannagh, avoiding the huge elephant in the room entirely and coming up with quite a dull topic.

'No. I never saw the need. I love Dublin and have everything here so why leave?'

'I guess you're right. I often wonder how different my life would have been under different circumstances. But then I guess everybody does that, and you wouldn't be who you are if things had played out another way.'

'Exactly!' Brannagh responds in a tone that isn't fully involved in the conversation which is when I realise that she urgently wants to talk about what we have been brought together to discuss.

'Tell me Brannagh, how are you?' I say with emphasis on the word *are,* hoping that this will provoke her to tell me everything, and I can just sit, listen and absorb for now.

I feel a bit stupid for how I have brought up the topic but then wonder how else I could have without jumping too far in; telling her how I saw her on Friday in such a state, wanting to run over, wrap her up in a blanket and take her to our flat to protect her from it all.

'I'm not too bad, thanks,' she says with an attempt at confidence which I can see clearly.

I give her the eye that only an older sister would give when they know the other one is lying or trying to cover something up, and she almost falls to pieces but is saved by the ring of her mobile phone.

Instantly, I can hear the abuse that is coming down the other end. A male voice shouting frantically at Brannagh who is saying nothing on this end. There is no room for her to reply because he doesn't leave any for her. I guess she is used to that lack of consideration. I can hear bits of what he is saying perfectly clearly, and he sounds like a psychopath needing to know exactly where she is and what she is doing as if he has done something awful that she can't know about.

I try to gesture words to her checking that she is okay and ensuring her that she is safe in my company and nobody will be able to hurt her while she is with me, but she just looks at me, blank with that same expression that I saw before. Her face is pale, and her eyes are filling at the bottom with tears that are just waiting to burst out.

As she pulls the phone away from her ear and touches the screen to hang up while the angry male is still raging down the line, I go round the table to sit beside her and put my arm around her taking her tightly into me.

'It's okay. You will be okay. I am here to help you now. I promise,' I whisper quietly to her which is broken up between the snuffles coming from her trying hard to fight back the tears and restrain the sobbing fit that she inevitably wants to have.

'Brannagh, does he hurt you all of the time?'

'A bit,' she replies and instantly realises what she has implied so quickly corrects it by saying, 'but it's not so bad.'

Her responses continue to be short, and her face loses any life that it was showing before. I realise that right now in this public setting, I am not going to get anything else out of her. Why did I ever think this would be a good idea to meet in a pub to discuss such a diabolical situation, I think as Brannagh presses her phone enough times to ensure that the phone call has been cut off and gets up to go to the toilet.

'I'll be back in a minute, I just need to freshen up, sorry,' she says to me with panic in her voice.

How does a relationship ever get to this point? I wonder in silence as I sip on my extortionately priced yet freshly smelling lemonade, only taking tiny gulps at a time to make it last for the duration of our time together. I wince as the ice cubes clatter onto my front teeth. I can't imagine James ever contemplating hitting me. Well, perhaps he did occasionally during our uni days when I used to take forever to leave the house each time we were going out but even I find that irritating thinking back on it now.

As I sit and think where we can take this conversation so that I will be a help to Brannagh as I always intended, my phone starts to ring—Aunt Eileen with the kids.

'Hello pet, I don't know how much longer you'll be, but you've got two very hungry children here, and Jack is missing his Mammy,' Eileen says, and I feel a cloud of guilt come over me.

I feel guilt for palming my children off onto my aunt and wonder how Mammy used to do it so much with me without feeling an ounce of guilt. I feel guilty for Brannagh not being able to have the discussion with me that she probably had planned because we are in such an open and vulnerable environment. I desperately rack my brains for what could happen next to please everybody but soon realise that I'll have to sacrifice one side's happiness until a later date. It's impossible to please everyone. I then realise I've not answered Eileen, and it's not until I hear her down the phone asking if I am here that I begin to speak.

'Yes, sorry. Where are you? I'll be right there.'

My stomach sinks as I see Brannagh, thankfully looking brighter and smelling of a perfume that I am familiar with but cannot put a name to, heading back to the table. I figure I will buy her another gin because she's clearly inherited her drinking from Daddy and gets alcoholic beverages down her neck at a rate of knots. This way I won't feel so awful for telling her to hold onto her thoughts until I find a plan tomorrow where we can talk properly and start to get some solutions in place.

'Are you all right?' I ask her with genuine care which I realise may not seem too real when I tell her the news that I'm needed back at camp.

I can see her brain working out how she is going to tell me how horrific the situation is. How she is going to start such a difficult conversation with somebody that she has technically only just met.

This makes my next move harder, and we begin our conversation starters simultaneously, but my voice comes out bolder so Brannagh allows for me to continue.

'I'm so sorry darling, but I've got to go. Eileen is stuck with the kids and Jack is about to have one of his deafening tantrums which we'll probably hear from here if I'm not quick.'

'Go ahead,' comes her simple reply, and my tummy hurts for her having to leave, empathising with her so much that my stomach flips inside, and my heart physically aches.

I give her a hug which lasts that bit longer than the average embrace and silently tell her that everything is going to be okay. When I have more time. When I consider the place of our meet more carefully.

I walk her to the river, and we head off in separate directions. Luckily, she isn't staying with Daniel tonight and is instead staying at her mum's so at least I have some comfort in knowing no more damage will be done before we next see each other. However, I am not convinced that she told me the truth.

As I walk away, I feel horrendous like I have just done the worst thing to date. My mind is going nuts over what could happen. The could-bes which I have always hated but more so in this moment.

I head to the spire to meet my clan and hope that Jack's spirits have lifted because right now I can't deal with one of his uniquely uncontrollable tantrums. Walking through the streets of my birth city, I remember being young and no troubles worrying me. A scenario very contradictory to the one I find myself in now. The busy city centre is passing me by, and I fail to notice the amount of people that are walking by me as I'm in a zone completely out of Dublin not with it at all. Even the smell hasn't changed and instantly takes me back to being fourteen again, just before Daddy and I left, when I was roaming around carefree without anybody knowing what I was up to.

I spot Eileen, Erin and Jack stood by the Spire of Dublin as we had planned, looking like three tiny dots next to the huge landmark. As always Eileen is ready with a plan because she hates waiting around which pleases me, as I can never make a decision. With the children I'm usually fine because when they try to argue against my proposal, I have the upper hand, but when an adult is in toe I can never decide.

She suggests that we go to a nice Fish and Chip Restaurant at Portmarnock, and we have the added bonus of her car which pleases me because I am just about finished with public transport. Our relationship is through. I have never had much patience with it, but in my current mood and after the drama and worry of the past few days, my patience is next to none. Eileen knows all the best parking spots and cheap ones too being on the tighter end of the financial spectrum, so I don't mind offering to pay even though this idea whizzes by me shortly after we set off with Brannagh firmly back in my mind.

Eileen can tell that I am distracted, and knowing that this is not a matter to bring up in front of the children she starts up a conversation reminiscing about the old days. The trips she used to take me on to the coast and how much we both love the sea. The detours we would take when both Mammy and Daddy had told her the route step by step, but we always fancied an adventure and then would get horrifically lost.

As we get closer to Eileen's chosen car park, I remember how free Dublin always made me feel with the sea being only three miles out of the city centre. I would love to have that in York. Sadly, Whitby and Scarborough are just that bit too far away, so I always begin to feel a little claustrophobic inland, though I do make the effort to take the kids more than most mothers would.

The children get very excited on seeing the sea, and I think we all feel relieved to get out of the city for a short while. Even Erin is showing that same childlike enthusiasm for the sea as she showed when we were on the train to London to see Matilda the musical back in May last year. It is great to see such genuine happiness plastered over their faces which brings a smile to my own face for a second before remembering how I left Brannagh. I know this is going to haunt me until I see her again tomorrow, but I had to make that decision, and my children will always have to come first.

We arrive and walk to the Fish Shack Café following Eileen's recommendation, and I instantly feel the weighty load lift off me upon looking out to the ocean. This has always been a favourite place of mine to be, and from moving away from Dublin until this day the sea has always brought me endless amounts of comfort.

On arriving at the restaurant, I feel relieved that it is perfect for the children. To begin with, I know that they are both big fans of fish but also if either kicks off, there's no need for me to feel embarrassed, as there will most likely be another child kicking off on the other side of the room. The fresh smell of the meals cooking adds to the solace that I am feeling for the place but certainly doesn't remove the terrible guilt that I am feeling towards Brannagh.

While glancing at the menu but all knowing exactly what we will be ordering—cod and chips with plenty of tartar sauce—Eileen begins her usual talent of filling every second of silence with words. Her conversation is so random, but it's useful to me as my mind is veering away from Brannagh, though I feel pretty selfish for thinking this way.

'Ooh those candles look like the set I got you for your birthday this year, don't they, Maz?' Eileen asks me, and I can sense the present test coming.

This is when relatives, especially Eileen, decide to subtly quiz you on what they got you each year for the most recent birthdays to test your memory and whether you genuinely liked the gift. The worst is when they bring up Christmas too and I have no chance of getting anything right. Considering the most recent years have been somewhat in turmoil, my memory is worse than ever, and I can't even remember what I got the children for their birthday's let alone what Eileen bought me for mine. Fortunately, Erin is more switched on than me and remembers perfectly, winning the test on my behalf.

The children finish their meals as if they haven't eaten for days, Eileen leaves her usual amount, and I can't face food due to the worry I am carrying for poor Brannagh, so just move my chips around my plate as if I am four years old and rebelling. Eileen immediately clocks this and suggests that we head to hers before going back to our flat, sensing that I am in need of adult company and support. Though I know she won't address any of the issues, I know that it's her way of making sure I will be okay overnight.

On arriving at Eileen's house, she lives by her typical Irish ways and puts on the kettle noting that a cup of tea solves any given situation, yet not stating this, rather looking at me in a comforting way so we both know that she is thinking it. I feel claustrophobic in the house, though appreciative of Eileen's efforts and decide to repeat one of my childhood habits.

'Eileen, you still have the allotment, right?' I ask her, praying that she does because I need to find some peace in order to think things through.

'Course I do, the corn are coming up brilliantly this year. Would you like to try some?

Probably not considering you've just eaten a load.'

'No, thank you. Would it be okay if I went there a minute? Need some time out, you know?'

Eileen says nothing and just smiles happily and sees me out of the front door, knowing that I will still remember the way as it was so important to me when I was younger.

Even the walk to the allotment chills me out massively, and though Brannagh is persistently on my mind, I have finally found space to think things through. I need to work out where we can meet tomorrow to have a productive time together rather than her subtly trying to explain to me how awful things are without anyone over hearing.

I enter the allotment gate, and I am instantly taken back to being nine years old. Eileen and I used to come frequently and helped in the community plot too. We would always be deadheading flowers, watering vegetables and mowing the grass after we had completed a sufficient amount of work on her plot. We used to sit for hours on the bench at the top of the terrace and look out into the long expanse of plots, Tommy's always standing out for its overwhelming but stunning amount of colour. He would win the prize for the best-kept plot year on year, and he would always have the tallest sunflowers during the hotter months too.

I stand on the grass for a moment, reaching down to stroke the resident cat that roams around daily before heading to our favourite seat which amazingly is still here. I don't recall the dry-stone wall being finished thirty years ago, but regardless, the place is perfect and just what I need right now.

I sit staring up at the clear blue sky on this sunny Sunday evening in one of my most comforting places on this earth and just think. I can't get my head around any of the emotions that Brannagh will be going through nor can I relate to her situation at all, and it's at this moment when I realise, I must go and see her now.

I look at my phone and notice a missed call from her number. After ringing back a few times, I fear that she is in trouble and thank whoever is in charge of this great world that I became technical in the stress of our meeting and saved her address under her contact on my phone. It's a different address to the step I saw her sat on, this address is her mother's and the one she promised me she would return to after I left her earlier. At this point, I don't care if I see Sheila or not, I just want my sister to be safe and happy. My sense of direction for this once extremely familiar place returns, and I catch the bus to Portland's Place.

Immediately, my senses kick in when I arrive outside the property and see the front door wide open. No cars are on the drive, so Sheila must be out, and after calling a few times I decide to enter on my own accord, however impolite it may appear.

The mud on the carpet, as I step through the door, indicates that somebody has been here and left in a rush. Somebody has been here entirely uninvited. Dread runs through me, and I hope that Daniel hasn't got anything to do with why this house has been left in such a way.

I don't know the house, but for some reason I feel most comfortable heading into what I assume is the living room first where I spot Brannagh's mobile phone face down on the arm of the sofa. She must be somewhere, I think, and panic that she has done something silly like overdose on drugs or something worse and head upstairs to try to find the bathroom or her bedroom. I understand that I am treating this much like the celebrity deaths you hear about, always being found naked in the bath or head down on their bed with pills and empty bottles of alcohol surrounding them, but right now I am desperate and will think of every possibility. I must rule every possibility out no matter how drastic it may seem.

After finding nothing upstairs at all to indicate any suspicious behaviour, I head back down to sit down, compose myself and make a phone call to the police. I slip on the top stair because my knees have gone weak with worry and fear. I don't know what to do and desperately need Eileen to be here but cannot put any of this onto my children who will undoubtedly find out if I involve my aunt.

As I head into the lounge, I glance into the kitchen when passing and notice something in there. I don't want to enter, and in any normal circumstance I never would, but something has been released inside my body which gives me the strength to do so. I scream at the sight before my eyes. My sister face down, her hair a matted mess and blood seeping out from underneath her where she lay. Lay dead beside the knife that killed her.

'Daniel!' I scream. 'You fucking bastard.'

Chapter 12
York, 1999

Finally, the day had arrived, and one which Mary had been looking forward to for her entire existence. She didn't show any embarrassment in admitting that she loved the idea of a wedding day and everything being about her. She wasn't the sort that would be described as self-obsessed; however, she did like attention whenever she could get hold of it.

The venue that Mary and James had chosen was stunning—The Merchant Adventurers' Hall in York's city centre. They had gone for one inside the city for ease of access but also because they loved the archaic vibe that York had. The wooden beams that ran along and down from the ceiling and the crooked aspect to the frame looking from the outside made the couple feel as though they were getting married in Tudor times. This was appropriate as the past, though Mary never liked to dwell, was going to be a theme throughout her design and ideas.

Since the day her mother had left the world, Mary had said that she wanted to modify her wedding dress for her to wear on her big day. Her dad had loved the idea and kept it safe knowing that when Mary had an idea, it stuck, and she was sure to walk down the aisle in the dress Anna O'Sullivan wore when she became a McDinton back in 1970.

The arms were the one part of the dress that showed its age, so Mary had them altered quite drastically by getting rid of the flare and having them tight to her arm, right down to her wrist. However, the overall shape was much the same fitting nicely to her slim figure until just below the knee where it flowed elegantly out into the train at the back. It was white, of course, ignoring the Catholic tradition and highlighting Mary's disobedience being obviously not the pure untouched virgin that women were supposed to be on their wedding day.

'That was a thing of the past,' Mary had said while laughing with her dad at the pub a few nights before the wedding, gearing each other up for the big day.

They both predicted how emotional it would be. They had been preparing their feelings for events like this throughout their lives. For the first few years after Anna's death Séan and Mary found every significant event difficult. From birthdays to Christmas' to Mother's Day and beyond—every event reminded them of Anna's significant presence not being there.

However, as years went on, they found each event that bit easier. Every event that happened yearly that was, instead it was those that were one offs like Mary's graduation and, of course, her wedding day that broke them once more. Every wedding is full of emotions regardless of the circumstances, but Mary's would be particularly so with the opaque absence of her mother both in the preparations and on the day.

Eileen had stood in for Anna on the morning getting Mary's hair and makeup sorted so that she looked as beautiful as she could be. They kept her look natural and Eileen had never lost her talent at up dos with hair from her youth, so Mary trusted her fully to come up with the perfect style to compliment her dress. It wasn't until they looked back over the wedding album and compared it to her mother and father's wedding day that both Mary and Eileen realised how similar the hairstyles were. In fact, they were creepily alike and them both wearing the same dress too made it feel like the past reliving itself.

Once Mary had finished her PGCE year living back in London with Séan, she decided to move in with James, and they both knew that it would be somewhere in or close to York. They didn't consider looking around the areas near to their parents, and on the day that they began their search they drove straight up to Yorkshire to start looking there. Between them they had saved up a deposit, and both sides of parents were happy to help out so once they found their dream-

terraced house on a street just off Bootham, they didn't hesitate to put the deposit down.

Séan was great during the process of the move, and because they couldn't afford much furniture, he set aside time to make things. He made a coffee table, some kitchen units as well as the unique sliding doors between the kitchen and dining room which they planned to bring to every house that they lived in.

Mary and James worked all week, and the weekends were dedicated to the house until it was all finished. They realised that it was a long stint and was taking up their summer weekends too, but the couple knew that it would be worth it. Usually James' parents would come up one weekend and Séan would visit the next so that the house didn't become too crowded because it wasn't very big, but occasionally they would all be up together and get a lot more done.

Mary's perfectionist attributes, that she didn't realise she had, came out during the process and were evident on the morning of her wedding day too. She had enjoyed every minute of the wedding planning from the day that James had proposed in the middle of the museum gardens one sunny July Saturday afternoon, until the morning of the special day in her living room with Eileen doing her hair. Jas kept making jokes about her punctuality and told her not to be late for her own wedding day. It would be a first, but everything was sticking to the strict timetable, so she felt that the timing would be perfect.

They had considered putting a marquee inside the venue but wanted the wooden frame to be visible so instead had draped bits of white material all around to give it a wedding feel as well as taking special care over the intricate details of the table decorations.

Mary wanted to keep the old-fashioned style but also give the room that extra something so that it was special to her. Eileen was artistic so had come up with a lot of the ideas, but Mary was in charge of all colour schemes, seating arrangements, food, music, and Séan made sure that there were surplus supplies of champagne, a job he always took a lot of pride in getting absolutely right.

The cake was a traditional three-tier style sponge cake that James' mother's friend had made and sat on the table at the front of the room where the bride, groom, best man, maid of honour and parents would be sat. The tables for the rest of the guests were dotted about elsewhere, with enough space for a large dance floor at the back.

Mary wanted to be involved in every part of setting up even though the event company had said that they could do lots of it, and this was when Séan saw that same frustration towards her perfectionist qualities as he used to notice with Anna. A task that should only have taken ten minutes such as setting up the tables before the decorations were even out of their wrapping, took far longer.

Mary had to place each table in exactly the correct position. She would then stand back and look for a minute pondering and shuffle a couple to the left and some more to the right. This went on for about forty-five minutes before Séan politely but firmly told her to leave that job to the professionals and focus on getting herself sorted. He had tried the same tactic as he used to try with Anna and just humour her to avoid frustration, but after too long waiting he gave up and had to voice his irritation.

As wound up that the trait of his deceased wife and daughter got him, it did also bring him some comfort in the sense that there was so much of Anna living on through Mary. They never showed too many signs of being overly close for the years that Mary had a mum, but it was times like these when Séan realised that maybe they were a lot tighter than they appeared to be at face value. Perhaps if Anna had lived on then they would have built a bond that showed outwardly.

Séan had booked into a hotel nearby to give the girls some space on the morning of the big day and to avoid sitting in the corner getting quietly more and more annoyed at their faffing, a characteristic that he had decided was somewhere within all females because it was so firmly within the two most important to him. Instead, he was due to the house at eleven to see Mary and the bridesmaids in all their beauty. He was given Jas's camera and was in charge of photos because the couple didn't have a huge budget, so anything that they could save on, they did.

'Don't you be dropping that, Séan, I'll kill you,' Jas said in a joking voice, but everybody knew there was truth in this statement because that camera was her life, and she valued it more than anything.

'I'm just trying to work out which button to press.'

'Daddy, hurry up. I would like an album to remember how great I look.' Mary butted in.

'We all look fabulous, love,' Jas agreed.

Séan loved time with the girls and had adopted Jas as one of his own while getting on famously with her parents too who had a similar relationship with Mary. He loved the humour between Jas and Mary and how they didn't take anything seriously in life until it was absolutely necessary. They were both happy go lucky people, and that's why everybody loved them, always being the collective nucleus to any social group that they found themselves in. They simply bounced off each other, and this was being perfectly demonstrated on the morning of Mary's wedding day, which Séan loved.

Eileen had sneakily packed her video camera to capture moments like that one to put together as a montage for a surprise extra wedding present for Mary. She was good at doing things like this and extremely good at keeping it subtle as she had done while away with Séan and Mary so many times. When they first moved to London and emotions finally hit them both during the Christmas holidays, Eileen took them away to the peak district having never been herself but heard good things and packed her trusty camcorder then. They laughed and joked having so much genuine fun and not knowing that Eileen had it all on film until she gave them the tape after which remains one of their most cherished items.

Eventually, Séan sussed out how to use Jas's Canon camera which she always used so sparingly, and Jas took over after he had captured the girls as a group to get some more of Mary, having already taken hundreds during the process of getting her ready. This was another bonus to having Jas as a best friend, a free photographer for your wedding day and all significant life events come to that.

Though the budget was small, Séan had splashed out on a white Rolls Royce to take the two of them to the venue. He realised it was an extravagant move and had checked with James' parents if they were okay with it, but he had got himself a great deal through a friend, and the car had a special meaning to the family.

Not only had Anna desperately wanted it to be her wedding day car but their budget didn't allow for it, it was the car that brought the couple together when they first met back in 1965. They were at a car show at a village outside of Dublin and Anna was sitting inside one just to feel good, her friends stood at the side laughing at her playing the part so brilliantly. Her hair flowing in the wind and her stunning smile encapsulating Séan's gaze. He was at the show alone with his parents, so needed something to liven his day up and knew that Anna was who would do that. He bravely approached her, and they got chatting never to look back again.

A thankful tear trickled down his face while reminiscing and waiting for the girls to finish fussing over Mary's outfit so that she was ready to get into the car. The car which had just pulled up outside of the house and looked even better in reality to Séan. He had wanted to keep it a surprise but then figured if Mary got emotional due to the relation that the car had to her mother, then getting into this state while on your way to the venue wouldn't be a great look. He didn't know much about make-up, but he did know that when girls cry, Mascara runs down their face and ruins any beauty that once was.

Though Mary's family had a tradition of being strict Roman Catholics—more on Anna's side than Séan's—James' family were totally non-religious. Religious beliefs had been watered down through the generations so Mary was conscious not to heavily involve religion on the day, though she knew she would be ridiculed if she left it out completely. Mary did hold certain beliefs but kept them very much to herself and occasionally attended Mass on a Sunday with her dad.

However, this was more for a nostalgic feel of her childhood rather than for her religious beliefs.

She was sure that members of her family would have their own way of bringing more Catholicism into the ceremony or privately pray for the couple because a lot of them still held strong beliefs and practised the religion. She also knew that Séan would have lit a candle at the last Mass he went to because that was the thing to do. He lit a candle for everything which made everything okay, and this was one of the best things that Mary liked about Mass. Religious connotations aside, it was a ritual that brought her so much comfort, and if ever worried about something or someone in her life, she would always ask her dad to take her to Mass to light a candle.

James was pleased and grateful that they had decided to keep religion at a minimum because he was a total non-believer, and it made him uncomfortable, though he realised he needed to accept it marrying into an Irish family. He had been to a couple of events with Mary, her cousins' wedding and uncle's funeral, and both of which made him feel alien in very different ways. The sheer business of the funeral, though lovely showing how loved the deceased was, was intimidating, and the lengthy service felt like chaos inside his mind due to not having a clue what to do. Mary found it funny as she thought she felt lost during these events, but looking at James and the blank look upon his face throughout made her feel so much better.

The feeling of intimidation returned when James arrived at St George's Catholic Church in York and saw the masses of Mary's family gathered outside. He instantly knew how much fun they were going to have during the day and throughout life with many big parties to come, but he also knew that if he made a foot wrong then he would have an army up against him. It was a good job he loved Mary the way that he did.

Mary arrived with a grin, filling her face and showing off her white teeth. Séan helped her out of the car to ensure that she didn't accidentally stand on the train of her dress and fall, showing signs of the champagne that they had already

116

consumed. The crowds stood outside of the church waiting for her appearance and cheering while taking photographs when she arrived, headed in before her so that more attention would turn to her when she entered, they knew her well.

Mary was so excited about the incredible atmosphere that she could already feel that she blanked out while the priest read the vows and waited for her to repeat them, but only silence came with her smile. This was until the priest showed his sense of humour by asking Mary how much she had to drink the night before, and she soon snapped back into the room.

'I, Mary Anna McDinton take thee, James Carter to be my lawful wedded husband.'

The priest was aware of the lack of religion on the other side of the marriage so he was considerate and didn't make the service too lengthy. The couple were quick to get back into the gorgeous car and be driven to the Merchant Adventurers' Hall where the party was to begin after some drunken speeches from Jas, Matt and Séan.

Everybody in the congregation was acting as Mary had planned, out to have a good time from the offset, and half of them appeared to be drunk before they had left the church. As she sat in the middle of the top table, she smiled again zoning out of the room and admiring how perfect the day had already been, as if everybody had learnt their scripts and were playing their parts exceptionally well.

Matt's speech was as witty as Mary had expected, and Jas surprised her with the emotion within hers. However, the biggest shock came with how she reacted to Séan's speech which was full of emotion as Mary had expected but started her off crying within the first few sentences. Full of great advice to the couple and ending with a poignant statement, she felt sorry for James having to follow with his speech.

'I had spent hours mulling over this task, and it was the most difficult part about all of the preparations which has now just been made one hundred per cent harder having to follow on from Séan's incredible words. I don't feel I can and would like to say a simple *thank you* to everybody so much for all your help, support and love on this day. Mary and I are so very lucky to bring two amazing families together to make one even more fabulous one, and I think the only way to celebrate is to get blind drunk and make some memories.'

A huge cheer came after James finished speaking, and Mary silently thought to herself how cool he could be, and that he had certainly got out of jail free on this occasion along with so many times before.

Chapter 13
Dublin, 2018

I freeze for what feels like a period that exceeds my lifetime, but I am sure is shorter and stare, stopping in the horror story of the moment. At least I hope it has been shorter because I need to take action as petrified and distraught as I am feeling. Whatever I had imagined, however horrific it may have sounded and as much as I felt I had been exaggerating it all inside my head on top of meeting my sister for the first time in person, I have never come close to experiencing what I am now finding out to be the reality of my life.

I am frozen; my limbs won't cooperate, and I can't move my eyes away from Brannagh laying lifeless on the floor. Part of me wants to identify her face, but the rest of me knows that it will only confirm that it is the sister that I never truly knew. The sister that I was about to create a loving bond with which we could cherish until our ageing years, building memories along the way. The sister that I was so close to saving but to whom I returned too late. The sister that has now died far too young, and I will always hold myself a certain percentage responsible.

I move my hand, still shaking, to my back pocket to retrieve my phone so that I can call the police. I am no expert, but the sheer amount of blood seeping out of her body implies that she is dead, so as well as needing an official confirmation, I need somebody to be here with me for support more than anything. My hands are shaking so much that I can't dial the numbers properly and keep having to delete the odd eights and sixes because I accidentally shake and press them too. Eventually, I hear the voice on the other end of the line.

'Police!' I scream in total desperation as the poor woman tries to evaluate whether I am being dramatic or have a true emergency. 'Police and an Ambulance, my sister is dead!'

I realise I have not heard a word of what the lady is saying as she takes me through the routine procedure in checking Brannagh's breathing, and it is the hardest thing I have ever had to do. I think she can sense my state of despair on the end of the phone, so she soon ditches the script and sends a quick responder on top of the two cars that she has already organised from my initial alarm.

On the arrival of the first response paramedics, a man and a woman, I have dropped to my knees and lay flailing on the kitchen floor beside my sister's corpse. They are very kind in remaining polite while asking me to shift aside so that they can assess the state of Brannagh and make room for the crime scene to be investigated. I retreat to the living room and take a seat on the sofa because everything is blurry and wobbling around. My vision is as weak as my bones.

I notice her phone is ringing, and rather than turning it over to see who the caller is, I panic and turn my back to it, facing out so that I can see partially what is happening in the kitchen not that I want to at all. In fact, I'd rather this all to be some sort of sick nightmare and to wake up happily enjoying a leisurely holiday with my two children in Dublin like I was two days ago.

Though my vision has totally blurred, my hearing has returned to consciousness, and I can hear mutters of medical language coming from inside the kitchen. This is when I think to myself that there is no point listening in because I know the outcome and hearing all that they have to say will only worry me more.

I press my phone and see two missed calls from Eileen as well as a message from Daddy that reads:

I hope you have all had a lovely day. I so wish I could have been there.

If only he knew, I think, but then I don't want to worry him. Not now anyway. I know that I will have to tell Eileen at some point in the next few hours, but until I have got myself out of this initial frenzy and spoken to the professionals, I can't handle talking to anybody.

The female paramedic enters the room and sits down beside me placing her hand on my knee for comfort.

'I am very sorry to be the bearer of awfully sad news, but I'm afraid your sister has died at the scene, and there is nothing we can do to save her.'

My reaction comes as I had expected, and I begin to wail uncontrollably into the chest of the paramedic as she holds me tightly instantly demonstrating the support that I am going to need through this. Still holding me close, she continues: 'Now the police are going to need to ask you some questions shortly about what you saw today, and the house is going to remain a crime scene for some time. Do you live here?'

'No,' I utter as weakly as I feel.

'Okay. We will also be providing yourself and any close friends or family who require it with some support through this, and we highly advise that you take any help that we can offer. Now take your time. I will stay until somebody else can be with you. This is not going to be easy for you. My name is Ellen by the way.'

What a lovely, genuine, amazing young girl, I think to myself among the more painful thoughts inside my head. As busy as she is and removed from the situation, she can still show her humanity and care to me—a stranger —and for that I feel thankful. At such a young age too, I consider as I come to the conclusion after a small evaluation that she can't be any older than twenty-five, yet she holds such a huge responsibility through her job and must witness horrific scenes like this one on a yearly basis, at least.

My phone begins to buzz again when I remember that I had told Eileen I needed space and was off to the allotment. She has no doubt gone looking for me, as I must have been away two hours or more now, so she will be worried.

'Do you want me to answer that for you?' Ellen asks me, again saying exactly the correct thing and putting me as at ease as I could be in these circumstances.

I know that I should be the one to answer the call but equally know that I will panic and end up silently showing the caller the state of terror that I am in, worrying them more. I look to the screen which reads *Eileen* as I predicted and fret. Ellen picks up on my anxiety and brings her body slightly closer to mine, putting her arm around my shoulder. With this gesture I nod reluctantly, and Ellen answers the phone.

As soon as I hear her professional jargon, I know that I have made the right decision in letting Ellen deal with breaking the news to Eileen rather than myself being a blubbering mess and struggling to communicate. I know that Eileen will be reassured knowing that I am with people who know what they're doing and who know how to deal with people who have just experienced such a trauma. Though I also know she will come up with a strategic plan on palming off the kids so that she can come to me as soon as possible.

As Ellen presses the screen of my phone to hang up on Eileen and passes it back to me, a policeman is stood at the door gesturing for a word with her. She leaves the sitting room where we have been sat to talk quietly outside, and I wonder what there could possibly be to keep secret from me in this scenario. I think I am dealing with enough, I don't need them gossiping about me in the corridor next to where my sister's corpse lays. I then have a word with myself inside my head which is a frequent occurrence for me and tell myself to stop jumping to conclusions. After all they may be fulfilling a nasty procedure that I'd rather not see or something else equally disturbing.

Of course, I was being entirely over the top, and the man was merely asking Ellen to keep me calm while they remove the body and examine the crime scene before taking me to the station to give my statement. Ellen tells me this while sat back beside me, assuring me that it's going to be okay.

'Can't I give my statement here?' I ask, wondering why I need to be constantly reminded of the seriousness of the crime committed. I can vision myself in the room at the station, staring at the four walls and forgetting how to speak.

'I'm afraid; it's routine procedure, and we must stick to it, especially with something as serious as this,' Ellen replies, in what I feel is slight agreement with me.

I suppose I will have to get used to seeing the setting of a police station because there is no way I am going to let the evil man get away with it. I decided this moments after witnessing my sister laying there, lifeless on the kitchen floor.

'How many years will he get?' I ask Ellen, surprising myself with my bluntness and jumping to conclusions but a comeuppance that must happen.

'Whoever is responsible will get the punishment that they deserve, Mary. You will have a lot of support through this, both professionally and personally, I am sure.'

I look up to the ceiling and stare trying to focus and stop the blurring but realise that this won't happen until my eyes dry from the tears that are streaming out of them. I think about Daddy's quote and always searching for the silver lining and then think of Mammy's wisdom in saying that a cup of tea solves everything. At least I will be able to have one when we reach the station, and I will no longer have to angrily stare at the kettle within the crime scene longing for a mug filled with a white and two sugars.

With all the thoughts and a few words passed between myself and Ellen, I notice that the large hand on the clock has gone around halfway and that the police are looking ready to take me over to the station. This must mean that they have removed Brannagh's body, and I am glad I never saw this procedure because it would have haunted me forever, yet I know that the scene I witnessed a few hours ago will haunt me until I die anyway. In fact, the only part of this that I can find any comfort in is the fact that Brannagh is at peace now, away from the abuse and torment, away from the fear that she so long suffered every day.

My legs feel weak as I am ushered up by two policemen and Ellen to the car that will take me, and I am racking my brains for how to phrase my statement to kick start this fight on a winner. I don't want it to sound like a competition because it is so much more important than that, but there is no way I am going away having lost. I want to ring Eileen to come with me but then don't want to put pressure on her to find care for the kids, so I leave it and hope she can get there in time. There has always been an element of telepathy between Eileen and me from when I was a little girl, and she knew if I was upset in my bedroom or in the pub. She knew before she saw my tears, and she would always find a solution to my worries.

As we drive to the station, I look out of the window and observe everybody going about their days as normal. People whose lives haven't just been turned upside down with a huge legal fight on their hands over the next however many years. I think how crazy this world is that lives can be changed in such a dramatic way and so quickly too.

My stomach feels even sicker while travelling, and I hold my mouth in case I spontaneously spew. Manners always being at the forefront of my mind, no matter how dire the circumstances, I wouldn't forgive myself for vomiting inside a police car. Though I am sure they're used to it.

I'll never forget when I was ten or so, and Eileen was taking Daddy and me away for the weekend as she often did, leaving Mammy to redesign the entire pub. On this particular journey Daddy wasn't well. Whether it was more hangover than genuine sickness I have never delved in deep enough to discover, but what I won't ever forget is the smell of the car after he had been violently sick everywhere because Eileen couldn't pull over quick enough. As thorough as she has always been at cleaning, there was nothing that would remove the stench, and so we had to put up with it for the entire hour-long journey.

We pass an open parkland with play equipment for children who are all happily enjoying the sunshine. Some are in swimsuits running through sprinklers spraying up from the ground. Their parents are watching them contently, taking photos to probably plaster over social media to tell the world about what a fabulous day they are having.

Sunday, 3 June 2018, a very happy day for some. It might be a significant date like a family member's birthday or somebody's wedding day or the day that a first child was born into a young new family. For myself now and forever, it will be a date of sadness, despair and regret. Total regret that I didn't say more to Brannagh in the pub; that I left putting my children first and didn't jump on my uneasy feeling immediately and return to her as soon as I knew something wasn't right; that she hadn't quite let on the full story and the level that the abuse had reached. I hope that in time I will be able to block out every detail of this day and use it as a comfort mark and opportunity to remember Brannagh and what we could have had.

We reach the station, and the police open the door for me, understanding what sort of mental state I am in, so showing care in their every action. I mentally prepare myself for what is going to happen in the next few hours and run through my statement in my head. They give me all the time that I need, not pushing me to speed up my getting out of the car. I take it very carefully placing one foot onto the ground at a time, making sure that I have strength to stand up. As I push off the seat to get out of the vehicle, I am made stronger seeing Eileen at the door of her car parked and waiting for me.

Chapter 14
York, 2004

There was something about turning thirty that was frightening to Mary, but she couldn't put her finger on exactly what it was. She had enjoyed her twenties, had a great family who kept their distance, but each time that they visited, they all had a blast, and she couldn't wish for a better husband. Just something in her life made it seem somewhat empty as if something was missing.

When Mary looked back over the last decade and remembered all that she had achieved and the places she had seen she felt a little more satisfied. She had graduated from university having met the love of her life there and gone on to achieve her PGCE year with an outstanding result to become a fully qualified teacher. A few years on, she and James took a year out to travel around Asia where Mary taught English and James did odd jobs for cash, and it had turned out to be one of their best years yet. The memories from all of the significant events of their twenties scattered their house in the form of photos and ornaments which were now collecting more dust as the two of them approached the big three zero.

She had spoken to friends of a similar age who had the same feelings, but nobody understood why. Jas was in a high-flying editorial role in London with a gorgeous boyfriend and keeping up with the extortionate living costs that came as part of the package of living in the big smoke, yet she still felt as if something in her life wasn't quite complete. James' best friend Mark had started a new life in America living in California—the golden state—surely nobody could be unhappy living in the golden state. Still, the conversations that

Mark had been having with James lately implied that he too was searching for something else, for something to fill a hole in his life, but he couldn't quite grasp what that thing was.

Working as a teacher, Mary loved the school breaks. Each day during term time she would perform the same routine to the point where things were beginning to become a little mundane. She would get up at six to walk the dog, be back for seven to make herself and James lunches while James made tea and toast and they would go their separate ways to work, both returning home about six in the evening to sleep and do it all over again.

They had a fairly full on social life, but usually by the time that they reached the weekend, they were both so exhausted that they often cancelled plans and rearranged, so they could spend the weekend building up enough energy to survive the next week. This was why Mary fully indulged during her breaks, though slightly miffed that James couldn't ever be with her due to work. Despite this though she would organise something each day in her diary so that boredom was never an option. Then she would wallow in self-pity and depression for the few days leading up to her return to the mundane, soon get over it and look forward to the next break. That was her life, and that was why her career as a teacher was the perfect career for Mary.

When she discovered that she was pregnant on the 31st of August in 2003, just a few months into her and James trying, she felt thrilled. Thrilled to suddenly have this huge change in her life that would shake everything about a bit and remove the monotonous. Her routine would go for a few years and her whole world would change being given a purpose aside from work and parties that she mostly cancelled at the last minute anyway.

It certainly was a mad world, she thought, while staring down at the pregnancy test and thinking about booking a doctor's appointment to be absolutely sure. So many of her friends had been trying for a good few years by the time Mary and James had the children talk, and nothing had happened for them. That was why Mary knew she would be keeping the news quiet for a while and only tell family members to begin with. As excited as she was, she felt it a difficult thing too, because they had conceived so quickly whereas other people, who were close to them, were having problems, so rubbing their great news in others faces was certainly not a good idea.

For the nine months building up to the due date, Mary was in heaven. Each weekend she scrapped sleeping for days out shopping for outfits or new bits for the nursery which she spent her free time decorating by herself too. She didn't want to find out the sex of the child because she had always said that she wanted her first one to be a surprise, so they had chosen a neutral colour scheme ensuring that they didn't go overboard with pinks and purples and end up with a boy.

Suddenly, her entire life was devoted to the unborn child. During the week she would spend her days discussing her excitement with colleagues and more than one long phone call with James which was mostly her speaking about what a great dad he was going to be. All the teaching staff would listen in sometimes indiscreetly too because they found the love between the two so perfect, even though they couldn't hear James' replies. Even the cleaners had the occasional ear to the wall; in fact everybody revelled in the young couple's happiness.

Mary's evenings were spent embarking on the decorating of the nursery and browsing the internet for anything new that she could add to her huge shopping pile while still talking at James who would be sat in the living room trying to wind down after a hard day's work. When Mary occasionally stopped to think, she realised that she had reacted as she had always expected, totally excitable about the prospect of becoming a mother.

Part of her had felt that it was down to losing her mother so young. She often thought about this and wanted to give to her child what her mother was unable to give to her. Part of her felt excited to give her dad his first grandchild who she knew he would be smitten about. That was a fact that Mary knew from the moment that she broke the news to him.

She had gone down to London by herself on the train to visit Séan one weekend. James was supposed to be joining but got caught up with work, so he couldn't make it. On the tube heading to his house, she couldn't contain her excitement about telling him, so much so that she had to practise on a few strangers first.

She became that person on the tube who everybody steered clear of thinking that she was slightly mad. She began telling random passers-by that she was going to have a baby. Blurting it out spontaneously at uneven intervals. Announcing it to the world with a raised, excitable voice. The strangers all nodded awkwardly and swiftly walked on to continue with their days.

It wasn't as if she was toning her elation down being fully aware of the fact that she was in a public space. Instead, it would come out in outbursts at random to those who least expected it. One lady actually screamed when passing Mary because her exhilaration had made her jump, and at that point Mary realised that maybe she was being a little over the top and needed to get to her dad's house fast before making another stranger choke on their coffee.

Eventually, she reached Séan's street and couldn't walk quick enough so broke into a run. She continued to realise that she was being slightly over enthusiastic, but it was something that couldn't be helped. She also was filming the entire episode on her new camcorder that she had bought on discovering that she was pregnant to record every moment from then on. She was filming that particular part so that James could feel as though he was there too, always conscious to make him feel completely involved as she had read books on how important this was during the lead up to a first child.

That was a huge aspect to her shopping trips—books. She had bought and read them all. From breast-feeding to bonding in the first moments and what not to buy, she had the lot. James' cousin had discovered she was pregnant just a few months prior to Mary and was in the same mindset about everything so had lent Mary the books she had already read twice over. This didn't stop Mary going out to purchase heaps more that addressed the same issues only written by different authors.

For the whole journey to London Mary had imagined a big reveal, sitting her dad down and telling him calmly. However, calmness stayed outdoors when she arrived, and she burst through the door, not having the patience to knock and blurted out the words:

'Daddy, I'm pregnant!'

His reaction came just as Mary had expected in a series of tears mixed with the biggest smile and tightest hug for Mary. They were both crying, but they were certainly tears of thrill. After all of the questions and Séan offering help where needed over five times, they simply sat in silence, just smiling at each other. It was a perfect moment that Mary knew she would cherish.

Next came the news to James' parents which Mary again did alone and on the same weekend purely out of the practicalities of being down south. Having stayed overnight with her dad, she caught the train to Ipswich where James' father, Ant, was waiting to collect her. Both Ant and Sally had no idea about the news that Mary was about to break to them, nor had they any inclination that the couple wanted children. It was a topic that had never come up in discussion, so when Mary sat the two of them down over lunch and raised her wine glass to toast the unborn child, Sally's hysterical cry of happiness and Ant's shedding of a few tears of contentment down the side of his face were utterly true.

'Oh, my darling. That is the best news I think I have ever heard,' Sally said minutes after the big moment. 'I never thought James wanted to be a father, but I know he will make a great parent. You both will.'

Mary instantly felt closer to the couple who she had always found quite stand offish up until that moment. She had always thought them pleasant people, but she never felt that she would be able to create a tight bond that she had done with so many other non-family members in her life. Ant was very similar to James, but he always had kept his distance which she felt was more out of respect to the young couple, allowing for privacy and space.

Sally, on the other hand, had shown an element of separation and coldness which Mary figured was just an aspect of her personality, and it couldn't be helped. She had always been okay with this, but as soon as she broke the wonderful news to the couple, she saw a glimpse of that bond being created in the future. A light at the end of a very long tunnel of getting to know them.

Everything about Mary's pregnancy went as well as it could have done. There was no sickness, her bump wasn't too uncomfortably big, and she had all the help around her. Not to mention everybody's reactions being just as she had expected as if her life was a performance and the rehearsals were going correctly to plan. Her excitement was totally undisguisable. For the weeks leading up to the due date, Mary's dad came up to York to be there for Mary when needed, and James' parents were on call in Suffolk, ready to jump in the car and arrive within four hours if they were required earlier.

As with many first-born babies, the due date came and went by without any sign of movement within Mary's womb though regular check-ups showed no problems, so it was just an eager waiting game for everyone. A further two weeks passed which was the furthest that they would allow Mary to go before they decided to induce her.

Having done copious amounts of reading around childbirth, the process of inducing a woman was something that Mary had skipped over and mistakenly thought that after she had been induced, the baby would come immediately. Instead it was over two days before things started to happen, and she was beginning to get seriously impatient.

After an eighteen-hour labour which felt more like eighteen years, Erin May was born a healthy baby girl. She came into the world at just after two o'clock in the morning on Friday, 14 May 2004, weighing 7lb 4oz. Luckily, York hospital was close to the city centre, so it was easy for everybody to get to. Since James and Mary's house was so small, James' parents had booked a room in a hotel nearby, and Séan resided on the sofa quite comfortably.

The birth was another perfect moment in the series of perfection that had so far been the life and pre-life of baby Erin May. The physical birth was something that Mary hadn't recorded on her new device much to the family's relief, but every other moment was logged. She even got the camera out moments after giving birth to capture the first sounds of Erin's cries and then to video each family member having their first cuddle. It was something to be joked about in the future, but Mary was truly determined to record absolutely everything.

Everybody accepted Mary's ways and went with it. They came in to see the baby, a natural reaction of pure joy initially for Mary then to sit them down in a forced position holding the baby and smiling to the camcorder. The surroundings all clinical and blue blended with the nurse's uniforms, but the baby looked perfect. One thing James was thankful for was that the video footage didn't capture the smell of the hospital because that was something that he hoped he would forget.

How she could be so energetic moments after giving birth nobody knew, but Mary wasn't any old person, she was Mary Carter, and that was just how she was. Her commentary throughout the filming made people relax, and it also made the awkwardness of it all hilarious, so they knew the footage would bring happiness to them in many ways in the future.

After a few days in hospital, Mary, James and Erin were given the green light to head home and start their new life as a happy family of three. James had been granted two week's paternity leave to enjoy in a bubble of happiness, sleepless nights and slight fear for the future.

As lovely as the couple found each moment—even the nappy changing to a certain extent—they didn't deny how scary becoming a parent for the first time was. They had always been honest with each other, and this was definitely a topic included in that honesty and talked about often. However, they were thankful to have parents around them who had experienced it and could talk them through everything.

Even though Mary didn't have her mother with her, she often talked to her for advice too which helped masses, and Aunt Eileen was on call whenever needed. These were all things that Mary was grateful for as she would stare at the new addition to the mantel piece, a photo of the three of them taken on day three of Erin's life, while Erin slept on her lap and Mary didn't dare move so that she wouldn't wake her.

Chapter 15
Dublin, 2018

Eileen's presence instantly eases the weakness at my knees, allowing me to walk a few steps across the concrete of the car park towards her. She is the perfect person to have here with me, I think, as I slowly travel the distance between us, not once considering who is taking care of my children.

Through the commotion of the day and for the first time since falling pregnant with Erin, the two loves of my life have moved down the rankings momentarily, and my sole focus is on the here and now. I feel dreadful about this and realise that it shows my deteriorating mental state, yet Eileen's calmness and strength showing on the outside, when I know that her inner self is probably shaking with fear, gives me the strength to go ahead.

The recent heat wave in Dublin has made the ground so dry that it feels slippery on the soles of my shoes as if walking on a wet decking after a downpour in the summer. It doesn't help that the shoes that I am wearing represent the energy I have for the events that I am about to go through—worn out and bare. I feel as if I am a little girl again, ready to go on stage for the first time to do a piano solo. As confident and determined as I may have felt beforehand, all of this leaves me, and I struggle to put one foot in front of the other. Eileen notices my struggle as she takes my arm, and we enter the police station, politely directed by the officers.

Throughout the procedure so far from witnessing the horrific scene earlier up until now, I am grateful for the police force and feel comfortable in their care. I know that they will do their best to attempt to make a very complex situation as simple as they can, and they keep reassuring me and comforting me along the way which is helping.

This kindness is continued while we are waiting for a private room to be available when Eileen and I are shown to two seats and offered refreshments as well as the officers time if and when we should need it. We both opt for a nice cup of tea following our Irish roots and sit in silence next to one another.

When looking into the mug to take the first sip of my warm brew, not quite milky enough for my preference, I think of soothing thoughts about Mammy, but by the time I have placed the mug back to a resting position upon my lap, I am back in the police station.

I begin running over in my head what I saw and trying to grasp every detail about it that I can while trying not to panic and scare Eileen with my distress. Through my blurred vision due to the chaos going on inside my head, I notice Eileen is resting her warm hand on my knee, pressing lightly to soothe me and show that she is here.

'It's okay, pet. You are doing the right thing. It is going to be okay,' she says to me in her warming voice that always almost entirely fills the hole that Mammy left.

Only for a moment, though, but I am always grateful that my aunt has the ability to do this because she is the only one who can. I say nothing and continue going over this afternoon's events in my head.

'You're in safe hands, and I am here with you, always,' she continues, reassuring me that she won't let me down.

I know all of this to be true as she has been my rock in the past, and I know that she will be that same strong figure again, but all that I can think of is what is happening inside my busy head. It is like my brain has been removed by a ball of mixed up thoughts and emotions. A ball just like those rubber bundles of elastic bands that you can buy from stationery shops on the high street feeling like you've made a useful purchase when you know that it will only remain in a draw until you eventually chuck it out. An array of colours and widths all twisted and tangled together to make a sphere. A completely pointless purchase because in the time that you spend trying to untangle the messy bundle, you could go out to another shop and buy the bands loose which are instantly ready to wrap around things. This tangled ball of rubber is what is currently bouncing off the walls of the inside of my head in the form of my thoughts.

I realise that getting the statement right is so important, and getting as many details down as I can is crucial for the investigation to begin in mine and Brannagh's favour. I'm kicking myself for arriving too late, so the culprit had fled already, but I then consider how much worse the outcome could have been if I had arrived in time. My mind continuously reverts to the idea that I have a firm inkling as to who was responsible, and at least, Brannagh gave me a good idea of his looks, so I can pass this information onto the police.

Whether they take it on board or not is another story because after all that, part of my evidence isn't factual at all and purely an assumption from my chats with my sister who I was only just getting to know. It's a second-hand perspective and simply relaying my interpretation of our discussions. The more I think about it the more I note that this part of my statement doesn't appear a very strong argument at all, but I am certainly not leaving this part out, they need to know.

I look up and to the side at Eileen who is subtly watching me with a concerned expression on her face. I want to relay all of my thoughts onto her, but I haven't yet put them in a comprehensible order for myself to understand, so there is no way that she will be able to translate them into any form of intelligible English. I can tell that she wants to help too, but Eileen has always been good at knowing how to act appropriately in every situation, and right now I think she is merely respecting my privacy knowing that if I needed to talk urgently then I would. It has always been as if she could read the mind of the person she is dealing with, acting accordingly to their needs, and this is one of her finest qualities that I love about her.

I remember clearly on numerous occasions when I was younger and in a row with my parents in the pub. I was always sent upstairs to be dealt with later because, after all, they had a business to run which was the most important thing at that precise moment and something which infuriated me as a young girl hungry for their attention. Aunt Eileen was always aware of this, as well as being a permanent part of the pub, but she would always know when I wanted to be seen or left, and she got it right every time. It wasn't a difficult decision for her to make as I mostly wanted her to come up and see me and occasionally would give her the look before being forcefully guided up the stairs. She would then be up within five minutes, and together we would resolve whatever the issue was. However, occasionally when the world felt really against me inside my innocent head, when I just wanted to be alone in my world of teddies and dolls, Eileen always knew this as well, so she would give me the space that I needed at the time.

I notice that my mind has been considering past memories as opposed to the dreaded statement for a while, and I get frustrated when I realise that the ball of mix-up is back bouncing around my head. Again, I am fully aware of being back in the gloomy station which is appearing even darker as my thoughts darken with it.

For moments that only last for seconds, my mind goes entirely blank, and even the surrounding within the police station blurs to the point that it almost vanishes. This is when I wish to wake up and pray that it has all been a dream. The type of ending that would ruin a film or book for me, but when it comes to a reality like this one, it is exactly how I would like it to end.

Eventually, the time has come for Eileen and me to be led into the private room. Though my vulnerability hasn't entitled me to provide a video statement, which I am very glad about because that footage would be sure to haunt me for the rest of my life, I have been granted the total privacy that I need. The case has been classed as one of extreme sensitivity, which I figure is most likely the way for any murder cases or those to do with death of any kind, so I am given as much time as I need and provided two officers to be in the room with me. One officer to note down my statement and the other I guess is purely for consoling purposes and added security, it's all routine procedure. There seems to be a lot to this *routine procedure*, and I realise how huge the police force needs to be to cope with going through the correct process each time that a crime is committed.

The room is just as I have seen on so many television crime dramas in my lifetime. Plain in décor and empty of things, only a table and four chairs as well as a water dispenser in the corner and a few devices that I predict are for interviews. Before uttering a word, I consider who has been in this room prior to us.

Maybe a serial killer once sat where I am sat now, struggling to come up with a plausible statement of defence to avoid being locked away for life. Perhaps a rape victim has been in the exact spot that I now find myself in, crying in despair knowing that their life will never be the same again whether the criminal gets charged or not. A mother may have sat here having just identified her son's body as a result of a drink driver hit and run. The anger she would have felt is unimaginable. I consider the mix of emotions that will have been through this room from people in all sorts of situations, and then I consider my own feelings and finally start to speak.

'Take all the time that you need, darling,' Eileen reassures me saying what I feel that the officers both want to say but refrain, trying to remain professional and not sway my statement in any way.

I look up to her and smile slightly, having uttered only three words. Three words is progress, I think, and I have got all the time that I need anyway. Everybody keeps telling me this. I think again and decide to begin the statement from my initial uneasiness while at the allotment when I first decided to go to her house. I must defend my own actions in all of this as well as Brannagh's vulnerability.

I begin even further back from the feelings that I experienced while in the allotment and start from leaving Brannagh at the pub to put the officers and whoever else reviews this right in the picture. My body already aches as it used to during exams in school when you had to write over three thousand words in one and a half hours, so you didn't stop writing, hoping that it would all be worth it when results day came. The pressure building from your wrists but taking over your entire body. However, this time my body aches due to shaking so much in the terror of getting this wrong and feeling that it's my responsibility to make a strong statement and begin this court case in front of whoever committed this gruesome act upon the sister that I never knew.

I explain in detail about the way that I felt on that day, which way Brannagh headed after we parted ways and how I went to search for Eileen and the kids. I can picture this vividly as I remember, looking back multiple times, knowing more on each turn that I was doing the wrong thing, but I was so torn, and my children will always be my number one priority, except for now. Except for now. I feel dreadful.

The feeling of guilt for my two children fills my veins, and the rest of my body is filled with guilt for Brannagh. It's for her legacy that I need to get this right. For her that I need to ensure the right punishment is given to whoever performed this awful act.

I take the officer on a journey of my steps earlier today, the conversations that I had with Eileen about needing some time to myself and the emotions that were going through my mind for the entire time that I was away from my sister until I found her on the floor in the kitchen. I try to describe the house at Portland's Place from the outside but realise that I could sense something wasn't right on my arrival, so I hadn't taken much notice of details. I can't even remember who I saw on my journey from the allotment to the house, nor what anybody looked like on the bus because I was so worried about what Brannagh had called me for and knew that when I found out it was going to be dire. Of course, I was right.

My body becomes weak as I attempt to discuss the moment that I witnessed Brannagh lying there, and every emotion returns strongly, having not left me yet only weakened. I begin to retch when the officer, whose job I gather is to console me, grabs a bucket that they already had within the room into which I complete the action and vomit. They are obviously fairly used to this happening as they didn't seem shocked, and Aunt Eileen holds back my hair while the same process repeats three times over.

I sit back into my chair, breathing deeply for a moment while Eileen puts her arm around me in a comforting manner and hands me a bottle of water followed by a fruit drop to get rid of the taste.

'It's okay, love. We're all here,' she says not knowing what else to do but reassure me continuously. It is working slightly, and I am able to speak again in order to finish the statement.

I can sense regret coming after leaving this room because I know that I would have liked to spend longer on the final part of my statement giving much more detail, but I wasn't aware of how difficult this would be and from the vomiting I figure that the officers will realise this. I know that regret is a feeling that I am going to experience a lot for the rest of my life, and I can only try to prepare myself for this so experiencing it now is a start.

After giving me a kiss on the cheek and a tight squeeze, Eileen takes my hand to guide me to an upright position, not knowing whether I will be stable to stand or not.

'Thank you, ma'am,' comes from the officer who has stood in the corner during the whole session not saying a word.

As we leave the room, everything slows down as if we are the characters in the final scenes of an award-winning television drama and the killer has just been revealed. Time slows; as the audience would react across the nation when who they thought was responsible all along is set free. Time slows as my numbness increases and I lean on Eileen for support both mentally and physically.

There are more people waiting in the corridor where we were waiting just an hour beforehand. More people who have come to defend their friends, maybe relatives over horrific crimes. Perhaps some aren't as bad. I hope not too many are as bad. Please God.

I look up from the ground when I see a wave of people passing so that I don't bump into anyone, though I trust Eileen completely to be my guide.

Sat on the chair where I sat before we went into the room is a lady who brings me an overwhelming sense of alarm. I suddenly feel as I felt a few days ago witnessing Brannagh for the first time. However, this face is one which I never thought I would see again. One that I left with such anger and hatred towards but now I feel sympathy for. I pass her holding my gaze for that bit longer than would be considered normal for a social encounter, and I think she recognises me too. I think we both know that we will be seeing a lot of each other over the coming months, and I think to myself that I must forget the past for now and focus only on Brannagh.

Chapter 16
York, 2006

As with anything in life as you get older, it seemed as though yesterday was the day that Erin was born, yet Mary had merely blinked and a two-year-old was running around the house. Mary had reached the age years ago where time seemed to be speeding up at a rapid rate, and years were coming around faster than they had done before, but she hadn't quite experienced the passing of time as quick as it had done with the first stages of Erin's life.

She had put most of it down to the mayhem that came with becoming a mother. The need to learn everything without knowing anything. The fact that no matter how much people with experience try to tell you and no matter how many piles of books you have read twice over, nothing could prepare you for what lay ahead.

The trial and error that was sleep patterns and the lack of sleep for her being constantly tired. She had moaned during her years at university about being tired when she had to attend a lecture at nine o'clock in the morning after a heavy night out drinking, but she now took all of that whining back because she now knew the real meaning of what tiredness was.

She became almost nocturnal, and as James would have to get up early for work the following morning, everything was down to her. He helped as much as he could, but there was little he could do, especially in the early months. Mary was aware that this would be the case and that men often found this part difficult, feeling helpless a lot of the time. When the baby woke up, she wanted to be fed, and it was down to Mary's bosoms to feed her, a part of nature that men were kept out of.

James sometimes got up first and tried rocking her back to sleep but the crying would only increase, and that was when he knew that all she wanted was breast milk.

For the first few months of Erin's life Mary would say that she got roughly two hours of good sleep within every twenty-four-hour cycle. If she then added to that having to keep up with the housework, make herself look presentable for constant visitors, make sure there would be dinner for James when he got in from work each night on top of feeding, bathing and burping their new born baby at frequent intervals throughout the day, exhaustion wasn't the word for it. It was as if Mary was paying for the perfect pregnancy she'd had with Erin's incapability to sleep and constant need for something.

This was something that Mary found impossible to decipher; she could never work out what her child needed because she just cried the whole time and it could have been for a whole heap of reasons. At the top of the list was always a feed which sometimes worked, but as soon as that was ticked off and the wailing continued, Mary was clueless. With that all said, though, she had enjoyed each part, or rather she could say that she enjoyed it all on reflection once the years had gone by.

Mary found dealing with a two-year-old very different. At the age of two, Erin was able to speak a little and quite well for her age, so communicating about what she needed was a lot easier. She could ask for food, say what she wanted to do, tell Mary if she was hurt or feeling sick and even occasionally attempt to tidy up after her extremely messy self. The difficulties still existed in the tantrums and frustration of not being able to do what her mind wanted her to though. At two, Mary could already tell that Erin was going to be clever and mature for her years.

From her experience so far as a mother, Mary had come to the conclusion that each stage would have both difficulties and advantages. She realised that even as a mother of a teenager, Mary would find certain things hard and post sixteen who knew what issues would occur, but she tried her best to see past these and focus mainly on the great aspects of motherhood.

So far Erin had made both Mary and James extremely proud. She was—most of the time—a loving, fun, sociable and clever little girl growing faster than they had anticipated. The couple also held an ounce of pride in their parenting so far because there had been times when they were close to losing it but somehow managed to hold it all together as they had always done before.

The help of their parents was a saviour, visiting frequently and genuinely enjoying time with their granddaughter. Mary was very grateful for this as she had heard so many horror stories of family fallouts down to the grandparents disowning the parents once a child is put into the equation, freaking out and not wanting to take responsibility.

She had read about one poor lady who was becoming a mother on her own without the support of a partner and suffered badly from post-natal depression. Her only glimpse of hope in the situation was the fact that she had a very close bond with her own mother who lived just down the road, so she was planning on leaning on her throughout, and she knew that she wouldn't mind. However, weeks after the baby was born, and knowing full well the lady's mental state, her mother abandoned her to the other end of the country. Mary found this extremely bizarre, and she was positive that it wouldn't happen with her family as all three grandparents were completely in awe of Erin, and thankfully, she was right.

Childcare was never an issue because Erin had started nursery for two and a half days a week which were the two and a half days that Mary had gone back to work having landed herself a convenient job share at the local private primary school on Bootham. St Peters was a well-respected school in the area, and not only was it highly practical for Mary but it also tested her teaching abilities and allowed a great deal of room for improvement. She was very happy when the head teacher rang her a month before her maternity leave ended to offer her the position as year three class teacher on a part time basis.

This setup took some pressure off James' parents and Séan to feel that they were required to care for Erin in the week which is why, Mary was convinced, they hadn't experienced the issues of Grandparent desertion that she had read about in her books and on Mums Net. They all lived so far away and there was no need for them on a weekly basis, so when they did come to visit, Mary knew that it was out of choice which helped to ease her mind.

Though they were never required to travel up to look after Erin, Mary did often hope for them to visit and was happy when they did because on her days off, motherhood became quite lonely. Erin was an early speaker and chatted away to Mary all day long, but sometimes Mary longed for adult company. After all, there were only so many times that she could watch *Underground Ernie* and *Numberjacks* which were played on repeat on CBBC daily. Most of the time, the episodes were ones that Erin was fully aware she had seen before, but they were her favourites, so Mary just went with it. Nonetheless, she did prefer to watch new material because it was that bit more exciting despite it being kid TV.

Loneliness was one of the unexpected side effects that came with the motherhood package. Mary had fully pre-empted the sleepless nights and smelly nappies, but she never thought she would feel as alone as she did on certain days. She would never have classed herself as suffering from any form of post-natal depression that were discussed in the articles that she had read. However, she did often think how easy it could be to fall into a spiral of depression during the first few years where your closest companion is a developing two-year-old and the most intellectual conversation you have daily is about another aeroplane that they had spotted flying across the sky.

As much as she loved Erin, work at the school became her sanity because for two and a half days she could seek adult conversation when needed and speak to colleagues who had children about the struggles that she was facing. Even at the school though she spent a lot of her time on her own teaching a class full of excitable eight-year olds while the teaching assistants took pupils aside for one to one, so she hardly spoke to them either.

On her long days spent at home she would get through piles and piles of women's magazines catching up on all of the celebrity gossip and even reading them twice over in case it didn't sink in the first time. She would find some juicy gossip and get all excited but then see that the magazine was from three months ago so that gossip had passed, and the celebrities were onto their fourth marriage. It was sometimes like sitting in a doctor's waiting room, filled with out of date magazines and a slow-moving clock.

She would try to keep Erin's developing brain as stimulated as she could by doing different activities all the time such as baking, painting and building variations of abstract art out of play dough. She'd even take Erin out for the day, despite their low budget, to get her to see and do things that some children were denied of because their parents worked full time and their nanny only did what she was paid to do. Yet through all of this excitement sometimes all she ever felt was alone.

Most of Mary's friends had either had children and gone back to work full time or hadn't yet had them at all so weren't around in the week to provide the company that she desired. Weekends were fine because everybody was available, and James was around if all else failed, but it was the weekdays that started to become a mental struggle for Mary.

James began to pick up on this, always being the caring man that she had fallen for and would take days off just to be with them which Mary loved. One day he completely surprised the two of them and went off to work like normal knowing that they had planned to go to the local park during the morning, so he knew that he would find them there because Mary's plans always followed through. He headed to the office, finished off some accounts for a few hours so that he didn't feel too guilty and then gave Mary a call which wasn't out of the ordinary because he often called her on his morning break.

'Hey, love. How's your day going?' he asked to check if they had left for the park yet.

'It's going well. Erin is being great. We've just got to the park, and she's in her element.'

Erin loved being outdoors, and the park was one of her favourite pastimes. It provided Mary with some head space too as she had always used walking or being out in the open as a coping mechanism in times of stress and with Erin being the confident young girl that she was, she would go off to play with any young children, so Mary merely had to watch from afar and relax with a cup of tea.

Viewing this behaviour from Erin brought a smile to Mary's face because it made her feel that they were doing something right as parents. All parents want their children to be sociable and liked, and Erin was already one of those children. She had no qualms about going up to strangers and asking them politely to play. Well, as politely as an advanced two-year-old could be. Mary would always sit back, consider Erin's future personality, and then begin to worry slightly at her confidence in speaking to strangers becoming an issue in years to come.

On this particular day, Mary was in one of these trances, zoning out and only focussing on Erin, trying not to get carried away with anxieties that she couldn't help nor solve about her future. Loneliness was lurking but not at the forefront of her emotions, and the sunshine helped to uplift her too. Suddenly she heard a familiar voice shouting from the car park and Erin was dashing over.

'Mummy, look. Daddy!' she screamed and jumped up into the arms of her father.

'Hey darling. We're off to the zoo,' James stated, with his charming smile spreading over the expanse of his face, and Mary felt warm inside.

It was days like these which didn't happen too often, but they happened often enough for Mary to survive the days on her own. It broke the week down into little chunks that she had to manage on her own rather than the long days all in one. Though two and a half days doesn't sound like a large amount of time, when spent alone with a young child it could seem like years to Mary and she would count down to the weekend which would then pass by in a flash as it always had done.

James would take them off to the zoo or the beach, into York city or another city centre and just be together which their favourite kinds of days were. The fact that James always seemed to manage to keep it a surprise as well made it that bit better.

Chapter 17
York, 2006

Erin had turned two in May, and Mary had purposely organised a weekday party. One reason for this was because her birthday fell on a weekday, but it was also a method of saving her sanity and an excuse to have adult company, a bonus during the week. She knew for certain that her dad and James' parents would be able to attend, and she would make sure that James got the day off work though he would probably want it to be a surprise. She also had a few friends that she knew could juggle work to suit so there would be a nice small gathering for Erin. Besides, she wouldn't remember it and no two-year-old needs a massive party, it was more for Mary than anyone, and Mary would be the first to admit that.

Mary eked out the preparations for the weeks before to spoil Erin on her special day but also to keep herself busy on the isolated days off. She spent days shopping for balloons, cakes, food, party bags and hats and then more days looking for presents for Erin. She never wanted to spoil her children but soon realised that once they were here it was difficult not to go overboard, especially when they were the first and the novelty was yet to wear off. She also ensured that there was plenty of bubbly for the adults as Erin turning two was definitely a reason to celebrate two years of surviving parenthood, so this was close to the top of the list of priorities.

When the day arrived, Mary felt exhausted, but luckily she had James, his parents and Séan around her to help with everything. There wasn't a great deal to do and not many people were coming it was just the struggle that she found with juggling taking care of Erin while doing other things. James' mother, Sally, was very good at noticing this and often took Erin aside to entertain her so she was out of the way. Erin loved Sally so it was a good time for bonding as well.

Though their town house in York was small, it was a perfect layout for gatherings, and before Erin they were always having people over for drinks. They still intended on having people over for drinks, yet these plans got cancelled due to tiredness usually. This time, however, the tables were laid, the bubbly was in the fridge, and Séan and Mary had had a sufficient amount before anybody had arrived, so Mary knew that it was going to be a great day.

Erin was on top form having had most of her presents from family, so she was occupied with them, and Mary was looking forward to seeing old friends that she hadn't seen for a while due to motherhood duties getting in the way. As she sat waiting for more guests to arrive, she paused to appreciate the scene.

James and Sally were playing with Erin's new toys on the floor. Erin was with them, of course. Séan and Ant were putting the world to rights over a cigarette and glass of champagne in the garden. The sun was shining, and they were in York, their favourite place on earth. How you could not feel total happiness in this moment, Mary thought, as she recognised, despite all the loneliness and pining for adult company during her days, how lucky she was. The scenes she was observing reminded her of the many parties spent at McDintons back in the day, and nostalgia filled her as she paused to reminisce.

Chapter 18
Dublin, 1980

It was a crisp Sunday morning, and Mary was in an excitable mood because of the party that was planned with all the family and friends that afternoon. Mary had been to Mass with her dad while Anna stayed at home preparing things, which she was a little annoyed about because she wanted to be involved with everything, but attending Mass meant that she was dressed in her party outfit already because she had to look smart for church. The sunshine made her mood even brighter, and she was determined to be helpful so that her parents could enjoy the party as much as she knew that she was going to. All of this was going on in her busy little mind and all for a party, just a standard party.

Growing up within the atmosphere of a pub meant that Mary was used to parties most weekends. In fact, she was used to having a party most nights, yet she always had to go to bed early because of school the next day or when the drunkards got a bit wild and her parents refrained from letting her witness that type of behaviour. This party was different though, it was a rare occasion when all of her family—the members that they liked anyway—would all be together, having fun, and Mary would be allowed to stay up.

Having helped Anna with the sandwiches, as much as a six-year-old could do, she was sent to pick the apples off the ground in the garden so that nobody tripped on them and hurt their ankle. There were always injuries at a McDinton party, and they were usually down to drink. Put it this way, if the guests were arriving at midday, then by four in the afternoon somebody would be dancing on the bar and somebody else would have fallen off and hurt themselves badly. They would be sat in the corner with an icepack strapped to their ankle and clutching a beer in their spare hand. This was a standard occurrence, but Anna always liked to make sure that any injuries that could be prevented were.

Mary decided to take a break from the collecting of the fallen apples and admire the day while sat on her swing that Séan had concocted to entertain the children during one of their other drunken gatherings. It was a bit skewwhiff due to his slightly tipsy state while building it, but it worked nonetheless. She swung slightly backwards and forwards while looking up at the gloriously deep blue sky with a smile on her face. What made this moment better was the smell of the apple crumble that Anna had been busy baking and the warm essence of the banana bread too.

Mary loved her house at weekends because Anna went to a special effort to bake constantly. She was a lady who couldn't bare waste, so with all the fallen apples from the tree, or the plums from the tree that hung over their fence or anything that guests brought into the pub for her—no matter how inundated she became—would always end up in one of her delicate treats.

Mary knew that Aunt Eileen would be arriving early to help with the setting up as she always offered her services and was the only family member that didn't get on Anna's nerves by getting in the way. So, one of the thoughts that was buzzing around the walls of her skull was the longing for Eileen to arrive because she knew that she would help with the picking up of apples while telling her stories about her latest expeditions that she always took herself on.

Eileen had never married but was more than happy with her situation. She had had boyfriends in the past, but none that lasted more than a couple of years, despite them all being good and healthy relationships. She was simply an incredibly independent lady and liked it that way, so no man could remain committed to her, as she couldn't ever commit to them fully. She had worked some years as a teaching assistant within a primary school, so care for children came naturally to her, yet she had never had any of her own.

She lived just outside Dublin in a country cottage with the most amazing views of the Wicklow Mountains and would take herself off on miniature adventures all the time. Whether it was to the continent in Europe for a week or walking around some new Irish scenery, the stories that she would come back with interested Mary hugely, and she hoped that she could accompany Eileen on these journeys in years to come. Sometimes, she took a friend with her, often she went alone, but either way she always had a brilliant time.

Eileen was highly artistic, so instead of capturing images on her dodgy camera that she couldn't get to grips with, she would always make a scrapbook in which she would draw the best scenery that she witnessed and create extra copies for Mary to store away in her special box as if she had been there with her.

It was the differences in Eileen's life to Mary's parent's that made their bond so close and special. Mary loved her parents dearly, but their life was the pub and Dublin city, they rarely ventured away from it. This was why Mary showed such a strong interest in all that Eileen did because it was so different from her normality and so it excited her innocent mind.

After a while of waiting and nobody coming into the back yard apart from Tessa, the Yorkshire terrier that had too much energy for her old age, Mary got off the swing and continued to pick up the apples from the ground. She realised that her bucket was getting too full for her weak, young arms to carry, so decided to take it inside and get another bucket to fill.

'Great job, darling,' Anna said to Mary, acknowledging the hard work of her daughter as she entered the kitchen.

She was painting the door from the pub to their personal space, and Mary chuckled at the predictability of her mother's behaviour. No matter when she had last redecorated or when they last hosted a family gathering, Anna always found an excuse to involve a bit of paintwork in the preparations. It drove Séan mad because he found it so unnecessary and a waste of time, but it was her thing, so he had to accept it and keep out of the way.

Perhaps she found it therapeutic, a way to relax before the guests arrived. Or she really did panic each time she had visitors and had a bit of obsessive-compulsive disorder about paintwork. Whatever it was, there was no changing her, so Séan just kept well out of the way and usually in the bar.

'When is Aunt Eileen getting here, Mammy?' Mary asked, longing for her favourite aunt to come bursting through the door.

'Oh, she's already here, darling; she's just in the bar with your dad.'

Not only did Mary and Eileen share a special bond, Séan and his sister were very fond of each other as well. It didn't matter how long they had gone without seeing each other, they always had things to catch up on, and a beverage in the bar was how they would begin every one of her visits. They could only have seen each other yesterday but would be able to write a book of things to talk about still.

Mary didn't want to show her upset that Eileen hadn't come straight outside to see her and had instead opted for some time with Séan, so she simply picked up another empty bucket to put the apples in and went back into the garden to pick some more. She often had the tendency to silently digest her feelings and would rarely speak of them, but most of the time she was happy inside, so this was okay.

As she picked the final apple off the ground and placed it into the basket ready for Anna or one of the chefs to concoct another pudding with in the week, she heard a familiar voice coming closer to her which brought a big smile to her face.

'Poor girl, have they got you working out here? You shouldn't be working on a Sunday!' Eileen said with a loud charm that warmed Mary as she turned around and ran up to her aunt to give her a big hug.

Jumping into Eileen's arms was usually how Mary greeted her, and it was often followed by asking where she had been and whether she had brought her a present back.

'I've not been anywhere this week, love. A pretty boring one for me, but I did go on a few hikes and found some incredible undiscovered places, so I will tell you all about them later,' Eileen declared.

She spotted Mary's disappointed expression which wouldn't appear obvious to anyone else, but their closeness resulted in their ability to read right through each other and to know exactly what was going on inside one another's heads.

'What we can do that will make you happy, though my little darling, is take Tessa out on a walk before the guests arrive?'

Mary didn't have to answer Eileen's question, her facial expression showed how much she wanted to go. She enjoyed spending time with Eileen particularly when her parent's attention was directed on other things. In fact, the time that the two spent together was precious in different ways to the both of them. Mary adored to be loved and while her parents loved her, Eileen's love came in such strong doses that Mary could feel it that bit more. While to Eileen, Mary was the daughter and child that she never had, so all of her maternal instincts that she had once built up in preparation for children were off laid to Mary.

Eileen had driven to McDinton's which she usually did with the intention to stay the night and drive back only once the alcohol had seeped out of her body the following day. Mostly, this would result in her staying a night or two more, and she was lucky enough to have the freedom to do so.

The great thing about living in Dublin city, and something that Mary had cottoned on to from a young age, was the breath-taking scenery which was only a few kilometres out of the city centre. Luckily, Eileen had the freedom of a car which linked the city to the rural, and she could escape when needed. She chose a range of different places to take Mary, and Mary thought she never let her down. Eileen knew Dublin well and was constantly discovering new hideaways in the wilderness, so she was never short of ideas.

They put Tessa in the boot of the car and set off for the coastal path, a fifteen-minute trip from the city centre and a friendly path for both children and dogs. On this particular occasion they were to drive to Malahide and walk the coastal walk to Portmarnock, a walk they had done before, but Eileen chose it for ease. They had plenty of time to spare as Anna—as always—was ahead with the preparations and enjoyed doing them by herself anyway so was thankful for Eileen to be there to entertain Mary while she did the finishing touches and had a large gin and tonic peacefully while waiting for the first guests.

Whether it was because Mary spent so much time with adults or an influence from her aunt, she appreciated the scenery a huge amount, particularly for such a young girl. She loved the places Eileen would take her to, and Eileen loved it as well. The range that was available to them surrounding Dublin was amazing. From coastal walks along the rocky uneven but beautiful Irish coast to stunning mountainous expanses in the wilderness surrounding the Wicklow range. They would get lost in the Heather and the Fern and pretend to be characters in Mary's favourite books or they would make up stories and each play a part.

Eileen was as fond of these occasions as Mary was because she was a firm believer in the importance of children and their imaginations, so she knew that Mary was getting plenty of exercise and development during these walks.

Mary loved to walk because it seemed to clear out her busy mind. She always had so much going on inside her head as any six-year-old would and was inquisitive about everything but never wanted to get on the adults' nerves by asking questions constantly, so she would store them away and just spend her life wondering.

The thing about walks was that these questions usually got answered in her conversations with Eileen, and if they didn't, then they seemed to vanish, leaving room for more pondering as soon as she left for home. She loved to be in the fresh air, to feel the sun on her face, the salty sea spray on her cheeks and sometimes the sand between her toes. She loved to see Tessa so happy finding the biggest stick for the littlest dog for Mary to throw for her. Backwards and forwards she would run doing the distance that Eileen and Mary had walked probably four times over. She loved to see Eileen so genuinely happy, an expression that she sometimes forgot to show on her face, and Mary never questioned but always wondered why.

The three happy musketeers walked the full four-kilometre loop in just over an hour which Eileen was pleased about, but Mary was completely oblivious to timings, as Eileen felt such a young child should be. On arriving back to McDintons, Eileen pulled into the tight car park for the pub which wasn't very welcoming as not many guests had cars and managed to find a space in the corner. She noted that she probably wouldn't be able to get out of it, but she could worry about that tomorrow, she thought, and would get Séan to manoeuvre her out. The car park was never full, so the fact that Eileen had just taken the final space implied that guests were already inside and plenty of them too.

Time seemed to stop a moment when Eileen turned off the ignition in the car. Instead of getting straight out, she paused as if she had seen something that she didn't want to see. Moments before they had been so jolly and Eileen had been telling Mary stories of her adventures, and those that she hoped she could take Mary on one day. The car was full of optimism and good energy. However, once they stopped everything changed. Eileen was staring at a red Volvo parked at an angle in the car park. It was one of the few cars that Mary didn't recognise, but she assumed it was a stranger visiting the pub and not the party. Eileen's reaction made her question her view, but she didn't allow it to taint her good mood.

Mary's excitement and refreshed mind from the walk showed all over her face as they walked in hand in hand, Tessa in Eileen's spare arm and into McDinton's.

Chapter 19
York, 2012

Mary sat in the garden of their new house in Huntington, a village just outside of York, considering how she had got to that position. With a large house in an expensive area of the country, two children running around quite happily and a husband who she had only considered leaving a handful of times which she thought was quite good for a twelve-year marriage, Mary felt that her lot wasn't bad at all.

Neither Mary nor James had predicted that they would wait so long for their second child, but they seemed to have experienced all the complications that they had expected to go through with the first-born, with Jack, their second and final child. Mary always knew she wanted two children, so there was certainly no giving up during the long process of conceiving Jack and then eventually giving birth, one month early and not short of problems.

He came into their lives weighing a tiny five pounds and spent the first week of his life with tubes coming in and out of his little frame. It was a picture that any expecting mother fears and dreads to witness, the sight of your tiny precious new bundle of joy, fighting for their life. Mary wasn't entirely sure about the job role of each tube attached, and she didn't much care only that they were keeping her son alive, and she prayed that he would live to see more days than she would. She had enough emotion running through her that she couldn't handle trying to understand the medical side of the horrible situation as well as dealing with her upset and worry.

Though the couple were prepared for the stages of bringing up their second child, they hadn't contemplated what it would be like with two of them, and they certainly hadn't prepared emotionally for the complications that could come with a newborn because Erin's birth was so textbook perfect. They were prepared for the nappies that they had experienced before. They could handle the late nights and lack of sleep. The crying wasn't so bad either, though this time around they had a six-year-old moaning about the constant noise and wanting their attention too.

Mary had often spoken to her mum friends about age gaps and asked those who already had more than one child what they thought, trying to get real advice from the ones who had first-hand experience. Most ladies agreed that the bigger age gaps were easier to deal with because you were dealing with different stages of growing up, so you would have a different focus for each child, not to mention the practicalities of the older child helping you out with the baby.

As soon as Jack was born, however, Mary completely disagreed or rather wished they had waited even longer for their second child. Erin had always been a big character as soon as she could make a noise, and Mary knew that she would always be a handful, though in a good way, of course. Erin's bold personality made Mary incredibly proud and secure in the sense that she wouldn't get bullied or pushed around in years to come. However, it didn't help much with the ease of having a baby and a six-year-old at one time.

As soon as James returned to work after his two-week paternity leave for Jack, Mary felt as alone as she had done before but now with two children, and she couldn't make sense of it. Luckily, Erin was at school until three o'clock most days, but this meant that the mornings were made more stressful. This time around Mary couldn't get up whenever Jack fell asleep or not get dressed at all because she had to get Erin ready for school and look presentable for the school run.

She didn't realise until she became a school mum how much effort went into the school run. Initially, she had thought the tough part of it was getting there on time and getting young children to listen to you so that you could leave the house with everything needed for the day having all had a healthy breakfast and brushed their teeth. However, it soon became apparent that there was so much more to worry about. There were mums there dressed as if they were going on a day out in London or those who just looked immaculate yet claimed they hadn't showered and had merely just thrown an outfit on.

In fact, she soon discovered that a lot of thought had to go into the school run, despite having a month-old baby at home, and she immediately felt the pressure. She would often think of her outfit while in bed waiting for Jack to wake and then while rocking him back to sleep, she would lay it out for the morning. Showers became unnecessary, but she had to look as though she'd had one as well as looking like she had just spontaneously been to the hairdressers and been shopping in a boutique on the way home which was obviously where her clothes needed to look like they came from, judging by the look of the other mums.

Occasionally, if she had family staying providing her with childcare for Jack, she would treat herself to an early morning haircut and smugly show up at the gate looking better than the rest of them, but that was very occasional. Granted she had sent Erin to one of the best private schools in the area, but she figured that school mums were a breed of human that would appear in most schools in England—state as well as private—and they were something that she had never come across before Erin began.

She felt like she was back at the university once Erin had started school and starting from the beginning in first year at that. She remembered going with her dad shopping on Oxford Street before heading off to York and she remembered spending a fortune, well her dad spent a fortune anyway. The pressure to look the part as well as having all the correct accessories from jewellery to kitchen appliances was extreme. The first few weeks of lectures weren't focused on the course content but rather whether you looked good enough to compete with the other girls for the handful of good-looking guys roaming around campus.

The school run had put her back into that obsessive mindset of looking at everybody else and considering how good she looked in comparison. She hated it. With Erin now in class one and James getting more and more annoyed at the irrational thinking of women, Mary had got better at coping with these pressures and no longer felt so compelled to compete though at the back of her mind the thoughts were still there.

Mary looked up at the sky and realised that her mind had been wandering as usual while sat in the sun in her garden. Jack was having his afternoon nap that she really needed to stop him having before he began nursery, and Erin played with her imaginary friends on the swing. She loved to sit and watch Erin grow which was something that happened all the time and a process which had continued throughout her life so far.

While growing up she had been a fast developer, walking and talking before her peers, and from then on everything seemed to happen just the same. She would come home from school with books that people in class four would struggle with, but her determination to read and be good at it was so strong that there was no stopping her. She would often paint things for Mary and though she knew it was a mother's duty to praise their six-year-old for creativity, Mary would look at the work and be genuinely shocked at the standard. Everything with Erin happened quicker than the norm, and Mary loved to be a witness of this.

She often spent her Saturday afternoons in the garden, especially sunny ones. James was always at the pub for a few hours watching football or rugby or any sport that was on which was just an excuse for a pub crawl around York's city centre, but Mary didn't mind because she loved the special time with her children. Even despite their large age gap, particularly at the ages they were, they did sometimes play together, or Erin would show her big sister qualities and teach Jack a skill or invent a game for them both to play. It was times like these when Mary felt that she had made it in life.

Neither she nor James had especially high salaries for the area that they lived in and to keep up with the school fees and the cost of having children, but Mary thought to herself that emotionally they were rich. She regularly considered this and thought to herself what was the use of a mansion, posh car, and a bottomless pot of extra cash if you didn't have happiness and love like Mary and James did. They were friends with some very rich people, so she had to keep grounded among it all. She never regretted sending Erin to St Olaves, and on recommendation as well as the experience of almost two years there she was very impressed, but sometimes she wished she was closer to Jas geographically because there was nobody quite on the same wavelength in her circle.

This particular Saturday was an extra special one because Eileen was due in any minute from Dublin and Séan would be driving her to York to see them all. In fact, they were probably in the car and heading up the A1 motorway, but she'd have thought one of them would have rang to keep her updated. She loved visits from family because there wasn't much preparation needed. Of course, she would put on a spread and make some effort to tidy away the toys and dust away some cobwebs, but she didn't have to go overboard as she would with some of her posh, more judgemental friends.

As if telepathy was a skill that Mary possessed, Eileen rang the minute that she thought of her.

'Sorry love, we got caught up at the airport with traffic and you know how your dad gets in it all. We won't be far away from you now.'

'That's all right; we're just chilling here in the beautiful sunshine while James is in the pub.'

'Good lad,' Eileen responded, and Mary laughed at the lack of support she got from her own family when it came to James' drinking habits.

She then continued to laugh at her reaction to the comment as she poured herself a large glass of Sauvignon Blanc while laying out the picky bits on the side. That'll show them, she thought, laughing while pouring a substantial measure of the good stuff. Though no effort went into picky bits, the effort looked as though it was there, and Mary's signature party trademark was to lay out plenty of nibbles which everybody always loved. Mary was really only conscious of their ability to soak up the amount of alcohol that was bound to be consumed at any family occasion though. She realised it was only Séan and Eileen, but the number of empty bottles around the place the following morning would look good for twenty drinkers.

While taking the last gulp of her wine that she had drank at a rapid rate to play catch up with the rest, James came bounding through the door, lovingly kissing her on the lips and smelling of Peroni.

'Guessing you won the football then?' She laughed, not seeing the point in getting cranky at the fact that he had avoided helping her prepare for their visitors.

'Rugby, darling, it was rugby. Though I wasn't paying much attention to be honest.'

'I see.'

James headed out to find Erin. He was slightly drunk and full of energy, so he was willing to partake in any of her fantasy worlds which Mary was pleased about because she could feel herself getting irritated by him before anyone arrived if he had stayed inside. She decided to pour another glass and take a seat so that nothing except relaxation filled her and irritation couldn't nudge its way in if it tried. Of course, as always with sods law she hadn't sat down for five minutes before the doorbell went.

On heading to greet Eileen and Séan, Mary spotted a pile of mail and quickly sifted through it in case there was anything that looked overly important or overdue. They were rarely indebted to anyone, and James was great at keeping on top of the finances, so Mary had nothing to worry about, yet on the rare occasion that she saw red writing, she would always make sure that they got to it straight away.

Apart from the usual junk mail offering pizza deals at the local takeaway and suchlike there wasn't anything that looked like it needed their immediate attention though one letter that struck her attention was handwritten and in writing that she knew only too well.

It was Brannagh, but she hadn't written to Brannagh in over a year. Why would Brannagh suddenly write to her out of the blue? She was so confused. She tried not to allow her mind to overthink, and she knew she had to get to the door as they had rang the bell another time. She tried not to allow her feelings to take over, but she couldn't help but feel slight regret for not being in contact for so long. She immediately wished she had started drinking earlier as she knew that another glass of wine would have made her feel a lot calmer. When the bell struck its third ring, she realised that she had already prolonged the opening of the door for that bit too long that Eileen would suspect something was wrong, so she opened it before suspicions increased.

'Hello, hello!' Came the loud and enthusiastic greetings from her father and her favourite aunt at which point Erin came hurtling through the house to jump directly into Séan's arms.

It took a simple but warming hug for Eileen to guess that something wasn't quite right with Mary, and she wished for a second that they didn't have a bond so tight that they were transparent to one another. She wished she could hide away from her feelings and enjoy drinks with her favourite company. She wished she had never written to Brannagh back in 1988. Then she didn't quite understand why a single letter would set off such a turmoil of emotion. A letter that could be so innocent and ordinary. It was as if Eileen could already read what was inside the unopened envelope. Maybe Brannagh was merely checking in.

Chapter 20
York, 2013

Saturday nights in James and Mary's lives had become that of millions of parents across the country—quiet and dull. The two young children longed for Saturdays to arrive so that they didn't have to go to bed as early as they did during the rest of the week. In the Carter household Saturday nights were spent in front of the television with some form of takeaway on their laps and a glass of Rioja in both James and Mary's hands. They had always moved to red wine by the evening as they had usually consumed more than enough white throughout the afternoon. They both needed to wind down after a busy and often stressful week of adulthood, whereas the children were only too happy that they didn't have school the next day.

It was funny how for the children this was exciting and the perfect way to spend their weekend, yet for the parents they just wished for the children to get tired and go to bed so that they could enjoy some quality adult time. They didn't even ask for enough free time to make love to one another, those days were long gone besides there was never enough privacy, and neither of them had the energy. Instead, they purely wanted space away from two demanding children constantly asking for something more, which neither of them thought was too much to ask.

They wanted to be able to enjoy their wine without having to get up every five minutes to get a drink for Jack or some more ketchup for Erin. They wanted to be able to discuss things without the constant butting in and nosiness. They wanted to be able to at least kiss each other without the kids saying how grotesque they were being. They wanted a

Saturday to themselves, but then they felt awfully guilty because these two excitable young people were theirs, and they had chosen to bring them into their lives when some people weren't lucky enough to have that choice. It was a very bizarre mix-up of emotions.

Mary often thought while they were chilling out watching the X-Factor, or some other light entertainment that forms the menu for Saturday night television, about how different her Saturdays had been over the years.

Most of her childhood weekends were spent in the pub unless her parents or Aunt Eileen had taken her away for a mini break. Her first teenage years in England were spent with her dad and probably doing much the same as they were now. Saturdays at university were spent drinking and partying until the early hours to wake up and regret everything the following morning. Though sometimes she and James would spend evenings just as a couple which all their friends found absurd because they were so young and could be so serious occasionally. Before children they spent their Saturdays enduring their friends' company and longing to get back home for some alcohol-induced bedroom romance, and then children came along putting them where they found themselves in the present moment and as they found themselves repeating week after week.

The takeaway they had chosen was Chinese. They tried to vary the cuisine so that the children developed a diverse taste in food, whereas if it was down to James and Mary they would have chosen a Chinese every week. They lived off Chinese food at university and had one only five minutes away on foot, so a lot of their student loan went solely on that.

It was where they both felt that their love for the food had developed because neither had indulged in it overly during their lives before university. Mary hadn't seen a Chinese takeaway let alone tasted it while living in Ireland, and their new attitude to life once they had moved to England meant that Séan tried to cook only healthy meals and a variety all the time, so Chinese didn't come into the equation. While James' parents had adopted this healthy eating lark too and never ventured away from only the freshest of ingredients.

Luckily, the kids weren't fussy, so they went with their parents attempt to open their horizons to new tastes and accepted the fact that they were only allowed to have takeaways on Saturdays unless Aunt Eileen was in charge then they were allowed whatever they wanted.

It was a very normal Saturday with the whole family sat silently watching *Britain's Got Talent* when James remarked that he had a headache which was unusual for him because he never suffered from sickness of any kind, and if anything, headaches were the rarest. Mary only showed some concern as he had mentioned it a few times that day, to the point that he had avoided going to the pub because it was giving him so much gip, and that's when she really began to worry.

Being the tough loving wife that she was, she would usually tell him to have a nap and get over it because that always worked. Apart from the odd cold which he would dramatize and have everybody in the house suffer with him, he was never ill. However, the missing out on the pub implied that he wasn't overreacting, so Mary's concern was present. She had noticed him holding his head throughout the evening, but he wasn't one for causing a fuss, so she knew that he wouldn't say unless it was really bad. For minor injuries and the odd case of man flu he was the worst patient, but when he should have made a fuss then he usually kept it to himself. It was a strange concept to get her head around, but she knew James so well that she had grasped it over the years. She merely kept an eye on him and continued to enjoy her meal that was beginning to lose its heat.

As usual Erin had demolished most of the chicken balls and filled the rest of her plate with vegetable spring rolls, covering the lot in sweet and sour sauce which Mary felt was revolting to look at; she could smell its artificial fragrance from where she sat, but she was happy that her daughter was trying to develop a diverse appetite. This left everything else to share between James and Mary with a little bit on the side for Jack who ate like a trooper considering he was only three.

Both James and Mary would laugh at these scenarios and how times had changed from when they were dating before children. They would laugh at Erin's obliviousness to the fact that she hadn't shared nor considered trying any other dish despite their efforts to persuade her. They would be amazed at the amount Jack would eat and, in the moment, they would smile at not wishing their lives to be any other way until the next Saturday came around and they would regret not getting a babysitter.

James continued to hold his head on and off throughout the evening, and the expression on his face became more and more fearful. He had been worried about anything head related ever since his Uncle Mick died from a brain tumour that he never knew he had back in 1995.

Mick was only forty-six and hadn't any inkling of there being an issue. He didn't suffer from headaches or dizziness and one day just passed out onto the floor at his home to be found dead moments later by his friend who had arrived to visit. James didn't speak about this much, but Mary always knew how he had found it hard to deal with. This was partly because he had a close bond with Mick but also because he couldn't come to terms with the fact that a life could end so suddenly without any warning at all.

Mary had clearly been more concerned than she realised because she looked at the clock to see that the time was now half past ten, and Erin was still wide awake with Jack fast asleep beside her. Her strict boundaries for bedtime were more relaxed at the weekend, but this was a ridiculous allowance, so she swiftly picked Jack up in her arms and told Erin to follow her up the stairs. Erin respected her parents and was tired herself, so no questions were asked as she followed Mary obediently up the stairs.

'Mummy, is Daddy okay?' Erin asked, having sensed the concern in the lounge. 'Yes, darling. He's just got a little headache; that's all.'

Erin's eyes showed that she felt it was more than a headache as did Mary's wavering voice, but she said nothing and went to the bathroom to brush her teeth.

'Are you sure he is okay?' Erin repeated when Mary was tucking her in and kissing her goodnight.

Mary paused a moment and smiled at what a caring little girl they had. For a nine-year-old, she was very receptive of the goings on around her and didn't miss a thing, even when nothing was being said. It was almost as if she could read James and Mary's minds sometimes, so they often had to be careful with the looks that they gave each other. She was very proud of this trait of her daughters, though sometimes and in situations like this one she wished she wasn't so switched on.

'He'll be just fine. Now you go to sleep, and everything will be good again tomorrow,' Mary reassured Erin and switched off her light, leaving only her moon shaped night light on in the corner of her bedroom for comfort.

She spent some time setting Erin's door to be open at just the right angle for her preferences so that she wouldn't wake in the night and disturb them but also to prolong going back downstairs because she had a feeling it was going to be bad. There was no reason for her to believe this, but something within her said that things weren't good.

'Go and check on him, Mummy,' Erin demanded worryingly, sensing Mary's lingering as well, and with this she took slowly to the stairs, her legs shaking as they descended.

Before heading back into the living room, Mary saw her empty glass conveniently placed on the kitchen side and shouted to James to see if he wanted a top up. When no response came, she immediately put the bottle down and ran into the room.

She found James on the floor fitting in a foetal position. It took her some seconds to notice that he was frothing at the mouth and vomiting profusely at the same time. For a moment she froze in panic, but adrenaline kicked in, and she dialled 999 before contacting anyone to look after the kids. If James hadn't have complained about the headaches, then she would have assumed it was a heart attack. Instead, she was worried that the same was happening to James as what happened to Uncle Mick eighteen years ago. The only comfort she could take was that he was actively throwing up so at least she could be sure that he wasn't yet dead.

Once she knew that the fast responders were on their way, she rang her friend Sarah for support and to come and mind the house with two sleeping children in it. She was surprised at her logical thought process in such an emergency. Luckily, neither of the children had woken, and she tried to keep her cries of desperation at a low volume so not to wake them. That would make a dire situation worse with two distraught kids added into the mix, so she hoped and prayed that they would sleep through but knew deep down that it was unlikely this would be the case.

Shaking in fear, she put James in the position that the paramedics had instructed and checked all that they had asked. At least she thought she had, but the room was spinning, and everything had turned blurry as if she had finished the bottle of red as intended, though she knew that none of it could be blamed on the two glasses of wine that she had consumed.

She sat by him waiting for the paramedics to arrive, pleading desperately inside her head that he would pull through.

'Don't die on me please, don't die,' she whispered in broken English due to the numbness filling her face.

The wait felt like it had been hours, but the responders claimed to have arrived within minutes, so Mary figured that time must have slowed drastically in the moment. She was grateful to have people there who knew what they were doing, but this didn't remove her fear for James' life. While they ushered her out of the room so that they could properly assess James and put him into the ambulance, she stared out onto the drive to see a fast response car and two ambulances with their blue lights flashing.

She couldn't make out why so many vehicles were needed but then realised it simply demonstrated to non-medical folk quite clearly how serious James' condition was. Her phone was sat on the side and its flashing with the incoming messages and calls from worried neighbours who had obviously seen the chaos on her drive added to Mary's panic.

Her whole head was spinning and flashing blue, nothing coming across as clear at all. All of her bones were numb, and she knew that the clinical smell of the medical equipment was always going to remind her of this awful night.

Eventually, James was rushed out of the house on a stretcher and into the back of one ambulance. It had all happened so fast in real time but in slow motion inside her head. She felt like it had been hours, but it had only been minutes because they needed to get him to A&E, and they needed to do it fast. Mary's senseless body climbed inside the ambulance with him almost subconsciously, and she knew—in fact, hoped—that none of this would retain in her memory for long because she was in no way all there.

After an agonising wait while the medics attended to James, the consultant came to speak to Mary. He told her that James had suffered a bleed on the brain which is called an aneurysm. He told her that they can remain stagnant for years, but things become serious when they burst and that this was what had happened in James' case. He explained that James was going to be in a coma for the next few weeks at least to assess the damage and work out where to go from there. He informed Mary of the certainty that if James was to survive, things would be very different, he would be a very different person.

She was confused as to how calm the consultant had been in his explanations but then realised that he had probably had many cases which mirrored James' so he was very used to it. How different was he going to be she wondered, how could the consultant be absolutely sure?

A brain aneurysm, she thought while sipping a cup of tea the following morning and waiting for Sarah to drop the kids back. As expected, both had woken up, so Sarah had taken them to her house to mask what had gone on selling the trip as a fun sleepover while also giving Mary the thinking time that she needed. Sarah knew that Erin would question a sleepover at half past ten at night, but she allowed the questions to wait until the next day.

Mary had never heard of an aneurysm nor ever expected it to be something that she had to deal with. She thought back to the night before when it all happened when they were wishing things to be different slightly and how she wished they never had those thoughts. As if someone watching thought they would give them different by chucking in a life changing, life destructing event such as this one.

She thought about all they had to be grateful for before this and for a moment pretended it hadn't happened, so she could express her gratitude for her lot once more. How could she be grateful now with the uncertainty of James' future and the struggle of hers? How could she begin to explain to the kids that their dad may have changed forever? How could they move forward and be happy? She took out her pen and started to write to Brannagh.

With these thoughts and an attempt to put pen to paper a tear ran down her face and into her tea when Jack and Erin came crashing excitably through the door. She quickly wiped the tears away, hid the pen and stuck on a false grin, disguising her exhaustion and upset while greeting her unknowing children.

Chapter 21
Dublin, 1984

Mary had always been a happy child. She was popular in her classes at school as well as within the family and among the customers at the pub—everybody loved her. She rarely had moods and was extremely polite, smiling always and being friendly, unlike some of her peers who were regularly grumpy and hadn't yet caught up with Mary's calm, gentle and extremely mature manner. In fact, Anna often had to comfort other mums while at the school waiting to pick Mary up in saying that their children too will develop the qualities that Mary already possessed, it would just take time.

Her childhood was a very happy one. Much like so many other children, growing up was full of laughter and imagination for Mary. From a young age she was capable of entertaining herself and was constantly making up new games to play which she shared with friends when they occasionally came to play. Mostly, however, her time was spent with family and adult family at that, so her closest childhood friend was probably her aunt Eileen who was the only one who joined in her fantasy world and gave her a lot of time and attention.

She had a tricky childhood in some ways because her parents had to dedicate so much of their time to the running of the pub, so she was often left unattended to look after herself which is probably why she was so good at it and so mature for her age. Despite this impacting on the speed at which she grew and her life being not necessarily too similar to her peers, Mary's life was a good one. She had friends, excelled at school and enjoyed family time while at home. In fact, everything in young Mary's life was going well and ticking along as any ten-year-old's life would do when some dreaded news changed her whole world around.

She was never overly close to her mother, but they did share a bond that any mother and daughter shared. The love was unconditional, and she consulted Anna about everything, more so when Eileen wasn't around to be of help.

Despite having to work most hours that God sent, Anna always made sure that she gave Mary a select amount of uninterrupted concentration to do her homework on Wednesday nights. Often Mary found this a tedious process, but she enjoyed spending time with her mum, nonetheless. Whether it was Maths, English, Science, History or Geography they always put in one hundred per cent, and Mary would get top marks in her class as a result. Her favourite subjects were Art and Music, so it was a special treat when these were the homework for that particular week. Anna showed her creative capabilities and made the whole process much more fun.

It wasn't only homework which Mary confided in Anna for. Mary was a thoughtful child, always considering large concepts which was another thing she would go to Anna for. Anna was much more serious than Séan could ever be, so Mary would avoid asking him about deeper topics and stick to having a laugh. She observed everything and knew possibly too much for her age through being brought up within a pub environment, but this meant that she was constantly full of questions about life.

She would ask Anna about relationships, why two people would fall out of love, how someone could be married but love someone else, and these were all spurred from scenarios she saw while sat quietly in the corner of the pub having her dinner each night. That was something which Anna disagreed with, but Séan insisted that Mary was involved in. She felt that Mary shouldn't be exposed to drunks and raucous behaviour, but Séan claimed it was all part of life, so she may as well learn early on.

This distant but loving bond made the news of Anna's breast cancer diagnosis extremely difficult for Mary. Anna had checked her breasts from a very young age, ever since she had a health class at school and they demonstrated what you would feel when a lump was present. She realised that sixteen would be a very early age to get cancer, but she didn't want to take any chances, so every time she showered, she would dedicate a certain amount of time to feeling her bosoms and had got used to how they changed during each period and other significant points within the monthly menstrual cycle.

That was why when Anna felt a significant difference in her left breast aged thirty-four; she wanted to seek help immediately. She booked an appointment unknown to Séan nor Mary and intended on going alone to see the doctor about her suspicious lump which was potentially growing inside her. When the day came around, however, fear filled her, and she asked Séan to go with her. The consultant immediately had a look of concern once he had felt her breast, and he booked her in for a scan two weeks later.

During this time Anna remained calm and hid all signs that anything was wrong from Mary, but she found this incredibly hard to do. Her worry worsened each day, but Séan kept reassuring her that everything was okay. She kept questioning how it could have happened to her, someone who regularly checked her breasts and was always aware of the goings on inside her. Perhaps she had missed a check-up or two, but it wouldn't have been by more than a few days because she was so thorough through being so paranoid, and she had kept on top of check-ups since her school days.

The process took six weeks of consultancies to get an eventual diagnosis and one that was so unexpected to the pair of them. Though they knew the news was never good, they had waited for the six weeks until they absolutely couldn't keep it from Mary any longer.

Despite the upset and fear of the unknown and uncertain future, Séan claimed that breaking the news to their little girl was going to be almost harder than losing Anna altogether, which they knew was the inevitable outcome of a stage four breast cancer diagnosis.

They had returned from the hospital both startled and in disbelief during the afternoon, an hour or so before they had to collect Mary from her after school club, so they had some time to take in everything while also prepare how they were to tell Mary. Séan made them both a cup of tea and cheese ploughman's with Anna's favourite bread that he had bought from the bakers that morning while she got ready and mentally prepared herself to receive the results. Not only did the two of them have to come to terms with Anna's diagnosis, but they also had to break the horrific news to their young daughter and console her thereafter. The couple knew that their lives were going to be hell for the next few months at least.

Anna had been diagnosed with HER2 Cancer which was a hot topic of research at the time. Scientists had discovered a new gene in rats which was found to be the cause of the more progressive cancer. Once detected, it could be treated with a mastectomy which was discussed between the consultant, Anna and Séan, but in order to do this procedure they needed to be sure that the cancer had not spread because that would make the whole process wasted.

'Should we not wait until we know more,' Séan innocently said to Anna to break to painful silence that filled the living room.

'You're only trying to avoid it, darling. She's an intelligent girl; she'll sniff something going on from a mile.'

Séan instantly realised the truth in Anna's words and knew that he was only trying to avoid having that dreaded conversation with his daughter. He knew that for everybody else during Anna's treatment that he needed to be the strong one, but he also knew that he was the worst candidate for this role.

Séan had always been incredibly emotional, and it only took an advert for a lost puppy to set him off. After his first childhood dog died when he was twenty-three years old, he swore he could never get another because of the heartbreak caused by losing his first. Two weeks later, he was walking home from work and saw an advert for a dog that needed a home. Two days later he had Jesse the Border terrier and has had a stream of four legged friends from then on after.

Anna's cancer, though treatable, would only give her another three to four months so after the discussion with the consultant about how aggressive the growth was, and even before they had checked to see whether it had spread around the body, the couple had decided on holding off on any treatment for Anna's sake. After all, it would only prolong her life on an extremely short-term basis while putting her through tremendous pain and sickness as well.

The facts didn't matter on the rainy November afternoon that Séan and Anna found themselves in. Nothing mattered because it wouldn't change the horror of the future, and the fact that in just over an hour, they were going to have to break the heart wrenching news to their ten-year-old daughter.

The room remained silent while they nibbled on their sandwiches, which were turning slightly stale due to the length of time it was taking them to eat. Sandwiches filled with their favourite ingredients that they both would usually devour in a matter of mouthfuls were taking them so much longer to eat. Their tea, a beverage that they both consumed enjoyably throughout the day until it was acceptable to pour a glass of wine, was cold. Even the room that they were sat in looked sad without any lights on and raindrops filled the windows, blocking the view.

'Come on, love. We've got to do it,' Anna exclaimed with a trembling lip but a strength that Séan was amazed that she could find within her.

Séan sat at the steering wheel waiting for Anna to finish touching her face up in the bathroom and grab her belongings, something that was a common occurrence on leaving the house. However, this time his head was in his hands, and he was searching for that inner strength too. He thought about if men could cover their faces in makeup to hide their feelings, but then he realised that as a man he was meant to be the strong one and not be showing any of his emotions on the outside. For a moment he felt he had failed as a man when out of the front door he saw his beautiful wife walking towards him, as

177

elegant as ever, and he realised he could never have failed to have once possessed something so wonderful. Even if he wasn't destined to possess her forever.

Tears trickled down both of their faces as they drove the five-mile trip to Mary's school, thinking that if they got the tears out of the way, then they wouldn't cry in front of her. Of course, they were wrong, and immediately when they set eyes on Mary waiting to be collected, they both welled up again.

Mary instantly sensed that something was going on as soon as she opened the car door to greet her parents. Both of them coming to pick her up was a huge sign but also how quiet they both were facing away from her the whole time. Granted, she would usually get into the front seat of the car so being greeted with a warm hug from her mum or dad was easier than when she was in the back, but she could sense some uneasiness nonetheless.

The car journey was eerily silent, so Mary just gazed out at the rainy countryside while they travelled along, thinking desperately of something to say to break the silence, but the more she thought, the more she struggled with conversation starters. Thankfully, as they pulled into the driveway, Séan broke the silence but immediately Mary wished the silence had remained.

'I'm afraid; we've got some bad news to tell you when we get inside, darling,' Séan uttered, and with this statement, Mary's mind went wild.

Had their dog been put down? Had something awful happened to Aunt Eileen? Was the pub-going bust and needed to close? She thought of all issues, mentally, physically, financially, but she never expected what came next.

'Cancer?' Mary asked through watery eyes and a voice that sounded as broken as she felt. 'Are you going to die?'

That was a question that Séan and Anna had clearly thought about but realised that they hadn't actually addressed until Mary put it so bluntly. They inwardly thanked her for showing signs of her innocent youth in doing so, and for the first time aloud since the awful revelation of the results, Séan admitted that his wife wasn't going to be around much longer.

Chapter 22
Dublin, 1984 (A Month On)

For the weeks that followed that awfully bleak November afternoon, the McDinton household remained sombre. Waiting for the inevitable was almost harder than dealing with it when it came, Séan thought, and Mary said very little about anything and especially about her mum. She hadn't lost anyone significant in her life so far which was the norm usually for a ten-year-old, so life throwing this at her seemed very unfair.

One Sunday, Mary woke up to find that only Séan was in the house which was very peculiar for a Sunday. Though the house had remained strange and against their normal routine ever since the bad news was revealed, this Sunday seemed even odder. She thought she had heard Séan and Anna arguing but just assumed that was in her sleep because they rarely did bicker and if they did, they kept their arguments well hidden from Mary.

Whatever had happened, Mary's intuition told her that it was something significant, so she decided to venture downstairs to ask her dad about what had gone on. As she descended the stairs to their personal kitchen, she could hear muffled sounds of crying. She was sure it was only Séan in the house, and the pub was closed until midday, but it was very rare that he would cry. Alarm bells rang within her jumping to the horrifying conclusion that perhaps Anna had slipped away sooner than expected. However, she knew Séan would have let her say bye and there would have been more family round at the house to support them all.

'Daddy, are you all right?' she asked, thinking that the obvious question was the place to begin.

'Hi, darling, we need to talk,' Séan replied in a weak and wavering voice.

He pulled out a chair at the kitchen table and checked the clock to see how much time he had before the pub was due to open. After he had given Mary an orange juice and some toast with strawberry jam spread thinly on it, he began.

'Now this is going to be very difficult for you to hear, especially now.' Séan paused for a moment to gather himself and quickly work out how he was going to break to his young daughter the news that he had been having an affair with his accountant for the past few years. How he was going to explain that he still loved Anna so much and cared for her beyond his control, but he was at the wrong place at the wrong time, and he made a big mistake. A mistake that he wasn't sure whether he regretted or not until he heard the devastating news about Anna's diagnosis. How he was to explain to a girl of ten how all of this can happen in life, yet it wasn't because anything was wrong with their relationship.

For the entire time that Séan was attempting to talk Mary through all of this, she was sat staring through him filled with rage and an image of Sheila behind him. Sheila came to the house often to collect receipts and bring up to date books to be stored away in the attic.

Mary thought about all the times she had smiled and been polite to this horrible woman. She remembered the times that she would help carry things and hold the ladder for the attic. She wished she had let it fall with Sheila right behind it, both crashing to the floor in a big heap. She felt hurt.

Once Séan had finished his flaky explanation and tried to give Mary a hug which was rejected strongly, she retreated to her room and got back into her bed. A while later Anna returned home, said nothing to Séan and headed straight to Mary's room knowing that was exactly where she would be. She got into bed with Mary and held her, both wallowing, and she thought that was where they would remain for now, Séan could deal with the pub.

Chapter 23
York, 2013

It was two months on since that horrific night when James' aneurism ruptured, the family's lives changed forever, and Mary was struggling to say the least. Not only was she having to deal with her own emotions and stress, but she had the responsibility of two very young children who were finding the whole situation difficult as well.

Her daily routine was filled with hospital visits to James who had recently been taken out of his coma and was suffering from posttraumatic amnesia and then returning back to normality. This would usually be after a big cry once she had got back to the car to get it all out of her system before attempting to keep on top of the housework and other jobs while also taking care of the children and keeping them as ignorant to as much of the goings on as possible.

Since the children were told about what had happened to their father in as simple terms as would suffice for them to understand the potentially devastating outcome, Jack had lost all the ability to speak that he had previously built up before James' accident. That worried Mary drastically, but having taken him to the doctor she was reassured that it was often a normal reaction of a child of his young age to such a trauma; and that he should grow out of it. Dr Ramsey suggested that Jack was a selective mute and told Mary that he had been an unusually early speaker anyway, but if he was still unable to speak in a few years, at an age where he certainly should be developing conversation, then there was a course of treatment that they could go through, and they would cross that road when it came to it.

That was something that Mary was beginning to get sick of. She was told it about everything in her life since the night of the accident, to face that when it happened, if it happened. All she wanted was everything to be back to how it was, and to have one more Saturday night with her and James longing for the children to fall asleep so they could enjoy some adult time together but the stubborn children remaining wide awake until the late hours. She really regretted ever moaning about her life.

Erin on the other hand was openly distraught. Most nights she had an episode of complete silence when she ignored any company that she was in, but after a while she came around and just cried hysterically into Mary's arms. Not only was she finding home life tricky, but she was struggling at school, and her behaviour, which was usually impeccable, had changed as she became more and more rebellious and argumentative.

Mary had meetings with Erin's teachers, but nobody seemed to have a feasible solution to the problems, so they all hoped that the issues would resolve themselves again with age as Erin matured. However, during each meeting, Mary thought to herself how mature Erin already was for her age and always had been, so surely this meant that she could cope. She then remembered how young Erin still was in reality, and despite her mature mannerisms, she should be allowed to react as any child of her age would to such a great trauma in her life so there wasn't much Mary could do. All she could do was be there to hold her each night while she wept which broke Mary's heart even more.

Initially Mary had wanted to stay strong and continue life as it was with a bit of lenience when she needed to go to the hospital daily to visit James for fear that each time might have been the last, but she had continued to work for the two and a half days at the school that she had done since having children. At first, she found the setup okay. In fact, it helped her to cope because for the time that she was teaching her mind was focussed on the pupils alone and wasn't able to wander to the darker places that it drifted in and out of for the rest of the time. However, after a month which in hindsight Mary felt was probably when the adrenaline had worn off, she came to a crashing fall and decided to quit altogether. The deal was to work her notice until the end of the autumn term, but even that became too much for Mary, and she worked her last day at St Peter's school on 19 November.

A week on from quitting work, Mary was in the car after another dreadful hospital visit, and having a big cry thinking that would help her feel a little better, when she considered how she ever coped with work as well. The emotion was too much let alone carrying the emotion of two desperate young children and attempting to keep as much normality in her life as possible, so how she turned up for work three times a week, she never knew.

The verdict on James changed almost daily, but the most up to date version was that though he remained in a coma, he was expected to make a full recovery within twelve months. Among many surgical procedures he'd had a huge operation where they fitted a shunt in his brain which drained the fluid. Everything was going to plan, despite everything being so complicated. They never said that it was going to be an easy ride, and the doctors and nurses were very honest with Mary about the stages that he may go through, and how heart-breaking some may be, but they did expect a full recovery and for James to return to a state of normality.

Mary didn't have the energy to show any sign of relief at this news because not much of her fully believed it to be true. She had read up on people in similar circumstances most nights once the kids had gone to sleep and barely any had the same fairy tale ending as the doctors and nurses so convincingly told her would be the case.

With Christmas approaching, Mary felt utterly overwhelmed with every aspect of her life, so she decided spontaneously whilst wiping away the tears and sorting herself out at the wheel of her car parked so frequently in the hospital car park to take the children to the coast for the weekend with her favourite companion, her aunt Eileen.

Before straightening herself up behind the wheel of her car which was parked in its frequent location in the hospital car park, she rang Eileen.

'Hello,' came the comforting voice of her beloved auntie, and Mary broke once more on hearing it. 'Mary?' The silence prompted Eileen to speak again, her voice less warming and more worried.

'Hi, sorry. Just having my usual moment,' Mary responded after a minute of silence and in a broken tone.

'More bad news?' Eileen asked, getting straight to the point as always.

'Not really. In fact, the news is quite good. They reckon he'll make a full recovery. It'll be a bloody long process, but they think he will recover eventually.'

'Darling, that's great!' Eileen said excitedly and made Mary aware of the response she should have produced twenty minutes prior when the consultant gave her the news.

'I know, I just can't feel happy. No part of me believes what they are telling me, and quite frankly, I don't have the energy for any more emotion. Eileen, I'm totally done.'

Eileen could almost feel Mary's tears pressing onto the phone, and she could hear the whimpers in her voice. She thought how hard it was to be away at difficult times.

'I'm sorry,' Mary uttered out of the depths of her sadness. 'Don't be daft, I just wish I was with you.'

'You can be with me this weekend if you are free? I know it's real late notice, but I just need to get away. Was thinking of taking the kids to the coast, what do you reckon?'

'There's no way I'm letting you drive by yourself. I'll book my flight now.'

For a split second all Mary's sadness vanished, and she was filled with love and warmth for her aunt who dropped everything to be with her and whose loyal spontaneity was a trait that she wished all humans possessed.

Though Whitby was always Eileen and Mary's first choice, they had opted for Scarborough due to more entertainment for the kids and shelter in the arcades if it was raining. That and the drive was a lot easier which was something that they had to seriously consider due to Mary's mental state and Eileen's pure lack of ever being a decent driver.

Eileen was due in to York station at around the same time as the kids finished school, so the plans couldn't have worked better. She was quite the independent traveller so wasn't bothered about getting the train from Leeds Bradford airport to York rather than Mary collecting her, and she always got the timings of everything just right; it was a skill that Eileen was well known for.

The children were very excited for their trip and even Jack showed signs of being happy. He made no noise, but his facial expressions and cuddliness towards Erin implied that he was on good form. Erin, on the other hand, was overtly ecstatic and had continuously asked how many days it was until Eileen arrived for what felt to Mary like weeks when it was only days. It was always Eileen that they were most excited for regardless of the excursion, and Mary wanted to keep it as a surprise, but seeing their faces constantly sad and glum, she broke the news early.

After a quick cup of tea, which was a staple to the Irish in any given situation, good or bad, they headed off for Scarborough. While driving down the A64, Mary was thankful for Eileen's company more so because she was chatting away to the kids who had a lot to talk about. Eileen gave them what they needed while allowing Mary to have some headspaces for her thoughts which were going off inside her head like all those firework displays on bonfire night a few weeks back which Mary had so wanted to take the children to but couldn't. She knew that she couldn't plan in her life as it was and that it was detrimental to do so, but she couldn't shut her head off trying to.

She was stressing about Christmas and what they would do, where they would be, whether by some miracle James would be home. She fast-forwarded her thoughts to the following Christmas and how many different ways the episode could have ended or continued on. She evaluated Jack's speaking problem and thought about whether he would ever be able to speak again. She worked out the stages that she would go through with him and promised to herself that she wouldn't leave it too long before seeking help. She assessed how she had been with Erin and whether she had given her the love and support she most desperately needed. At not one point did she consider herself.

They arrived at the same bed and breakfast in Scarborough as they had always stayed at since Mary and James' university days, and Mary felt a strong sense of nostalgia. The sea always brought this on and reminded her of her childhood in Ireland, but this time the feeling was increased with the huge link that the place had to James and their relationship.

The staff hadn't changed over the years, so they greeted them as good friends rather than guests and after taking their bags off them they sat them down for a refreshment.

Mary was reluctant to have a glass of wine in case it brought out all her inner angst but realised that the force from Tony would be strong as Mary had never turned away alcohol for the years that they had known each other. Within ten minutes she was sipping on a large glass of Sauvignon, and for the first time since everything had gone on, she felt that instant melting feeling inside, as if all her worries were vanishing for the time it took her to finish the bottle at least. Whether it was being in the company of old friends, her aunt or being by the sea she didn't know, but she was loving how she felt in the moment.

The children looked exhausted which was something that Mary was glad to have noticed as for so long she had been wrapped up in her worries that their needs had been overlooked, though she cared so much.

'Come on guys, you should go to bed.'

'But we're not tired,' came the stern reply from Erin.

'Okay, Eileen and I shall finish this glass, and then we shall head upstairs so you can sleep when you're ready.'

There was no way they were going to sacrifice their wine, but they still wanted to look like responsible and caring adults to the children.

Erin continued chattering away to Eileen as if they were trying to convince Mary of her lack of tiredness and Jack's facial expressions were as close as he could get to chatting, but he was trying his best.

'Do you want to go for a walk?' Tony asked, picking up on Mary's blank look.

'That would be lovely. Eileen, do you mind?'

'Not at all, darling. Go for it. We'll probably still be here when you get back!' She rolled her eyes jokingly at Erin's talkative ways.

The two of them headed out of the B&B and down the hill towards the sea. As they got closer to the water Mary sensed the freedom and comfort that the space always brought her, but she couldn't shake the thoughts spiralling within her head. It was as if an earthquake happened in Scarborough and all the rubble from the houses bounced down the hilly landscape and onto the beach. This rubbly chaos was her head. It was mayhem.

'I was sorry to hear the awful news about James, Mary,' Tony said in a warming tone.

'Thanks,' she replied, not wanting to say too much knowing that she would burst into tears.

Tony sensed this and remained silent for the trip to the beach, occasionally touching her arm affectionately to console her but feeling uncomfortable about how to deal with the situation. When they reached the beach, Mary stopped in her stride and looked out at the water. It was dark, of course, it was always dark in November, but luckily, it wasn't raining which would have brought the mood down somewhat. She took a deep breath in and at the same time looked up to the sky which had just a few stars in it and smelt the air.

'Sorry, Tony, do you mind if I have this moment to myself?'

'Course,' Tony said understandingly. 'I should probably get back to help Gem anyway!'

He finished with an upbeat statement so that Mary wouldn't feel bad for her request, and so she was glad to have asked. She needed time to properly process everything that had happened without children to look after, a job to keep committed to, house chores to complete and a normal life to upkeep.

As she walked closer to the water, the tears that she had expected began to trickle down her face. With this movement, some of her thoughts lessened, so she allowed herself to let go, and when she reached the water, she knelt just at the shoreline and started to wail in true film star style. Sometimes the tide came just over her knees, the cold temperature reminding her that the moment was real, but mostly, it just missed her. She didn't even have time to look around to see if anybody was there to witness her despair. She didn't much care.

Chapter 24
Dublin, 2018

It is now two months on from that dreaded day which I keep playing over in my mind like a horror story but one which I truly lived. Though I would never choose to select horror as the genre for our film on a Saturday night, my comfort has always been that it's not real, and then once the film is over, I am soothed to remember that my life is far from what I just watched. However, now I can relate to some of the plot lines, and I can no longer come away from virtual worlds to the comfort of my own because my own, currently, is not very comfortable at all.

Daddy has been great throughout the process minding the children and not totally losing his patience with me. We remained in Dublin for a fortnight after Brannagh's death, and I could have remained for longer, but then I knew I had to get the children back to some sort of normality regardless of what I needed to do for myself, so I had Daddy move in with us in York so that he could be on call whenever I needed him.

Now that I am not so disorientated with life, and I have regained some form of consciousness, I can tell that he was seeing so many signs of Mammy within my actions and how I have reacted to the events of the past few months. He has never mentioned it to my face, but I can physically see him biting his tongue sometimes, and when Eileen was over, she had to slap him a number of times when he became unaware of how obvious he was being. Though he has always supported me and continues to do so, Daddy has never been comfortable about how to appropriately act in many scenarios, and the past month has certainly been one of those.

Through all of the trauma and upset, what I am about to do is what I have feared the most. I know that I can count on Eileen's support from the moment that I step off the plane at Dublin airport until boarding it again when I leave, but I am petrified of everything that is going to happen in between. With Daddy minding the kids, who thankfully haven't interrogated me too much about what has been going on, I have one less thing to worry about knowing that they are in safe hands while I attempt to sort this mess out. Today, I fly to Dublin to see the lady that I felt so much hatred towards back when I was ten, but who now I can't help but pity, and who I now must be a support to no matter what my emotions are telling me inside. I am no comparison. I keep telling myself: she must be utterly destroyed.

In the taxi on the way to the airport, I am filled with every emotion I think I have ever felt plus some extras thrown in there that I have never experienced before. My sickness, I pretend to the driver, is due to travel, but really it's down to the turmoil of emotions going on inside of me. No human is built for this, I say inwardly as the driver gets into the correct lane for passenger drop-off, and I run through in my head the checklist of everything I need, something that usually comes easily to my organised self, but today is a huge struggle with all the other thoughts bashing around my head.

'Thank you so much,' I say in desperation, giving the driver a generous tip but really wanting to hug him and cry on his shoulder for hours to take away some of my pain.

The journey is one that I have done so many times recently that it has become as familiar to me as hopping on the local bus service into York city when I can't be doing with the city traffic. I walk through security and to the departure lounge like a businesswoman who travels daily, but inside I am crumbling. I decide that a cup of tea will help calm my inner volcano of anxieties but then look at my watch to see that it is half past one, so I decide that something stronger will do a better job of fixing me, instantly scrapping my drinking ban of the last few years. It will only fix me provisionally, I note, keeping a strong head through it all and attempting to stay in

190

control. A brief fix is better than the non-stop sickness that I have felt continuously since I witnessed Brannagh's lifeless body, splayed out on the kitchen floor. I still can't believe it.

While gulping my large glass of Sauvignon Blanc which is going down far too fast to remain looking sophisticated, I look around me at all of the people and wish to be in anyone else's shoes but my own. I simply don't know what I am going to say to Sheila or how I am going to feel inside when I see her. After all, her daughter may have died under horrendous circumstances, but she still took Daddy away from my Mammy, so the vengeance towards her is still going to be there.

Then I remember how strong I must be and how we are, in this case, on the same side, so we need to forget the past and focus on getting our victory. I remember that I need to be very mature about this situation and think about my every action before performing it, from greeting her when we meet to everything else that follows. I remember that Auntie Eileen will be there and will remain with me the entire way.

I continue to take in my surroundings to try to remove myself from my life for a moment and just stare aimlessly into space. Like watching people but not actually taking anything in nor thinking about anyone. My mind has other intentions, though, and continues to evaluate everything over and over inside my head. I wish that my flight was longer so that I could at least knock myself out with a sleeping tablet and copious amounts of wine for the entire duration of the flight, but an hour doesn't give me enough time to do this. Besides, when I arrive, I need to be awake and alert to prepare myself for what is to come.

I text Eileen to say that I am safely at the airport and about to board my flight and sign off with *get the vino in the fridge* trying to input a slice of normality into my day, yet she brings me right back to earth with her reply: *are you okay?* I know that she's only showing her care and how worried she is for my welfare, but part of me wishes she had played along with my false pretence, even just for a minute.

I order another large glass seeing that the *go to gate* sign is yet to come up on the notice board, and judging by the speed at which I consumed the last one, I know I will have time for another. Oh, I have missed it. For once in my life though wine isn't having that usual soothing effect. That first sip has always had the ability to release any tensions within me and allow for all my worries to float away until the sober morning, yet this time none of that is happening. In fact, I think my worries are being amplified with every sip. Maybe I should never have given it up in the first place.

I look down at my mother's ring on my finger and fidget with that a while, moving it round, round, and rubbing the ruby as if I were holding my Mammy's hand for comfort.

'If only you had lived,' I say quietly to myself hoping that she can hear me. 'Things would have been so much better.'

I consider how different my life could have been if Mammy hadn't been diagnosed with cancer so early and I could have had more time with her. We would never have moved to England, I'm sure, and perhaps Daddy would never have had the affair. Even if he had done, we may never have found out, so there would have been no reason for me to feel urged to create a connection with my half-sister, and I wouldn't be in this diabolical mess right now.

I quickly snap out of this way of thinking because running over my past, considering the could-bes and what-ifs, isn't going to change the here and now, so I need to be strong and get through it. Like most things in life, this is a lot easier said than done though, and the only thing keeping me in the departure lounge awaiting my flight is knowing that I will be in a tight loving embrace with my favourite Auntie Eileen in just over two hours.

I look at my glass of wine and feel ashamed at how much is still left seeing as the *go to gate* sign has now appeared. Not wanting to waste a drop and showing my lack of elegance, I gulp the entire contents, pick up my bag, grab the handle of my suitcase and strut off to gate number forty-one, pretending that I have everything in order while falling apart inside.

Again, while sat on the plane waiting for lift off, I look around me and assess the different circumstances that I feel everyone is facing. The man to my left has his laptop open on a spreadsheet, so I figure that he is obviously off on a business trip, and judging by his lack of will to converse with me as I ask him to allow me into my seat, I conclude that he is a very boring and lonely man, putting work above all pleasures in life.

The lady in front of me is sat with a screaming child on her lap to which I can strongly relate to, and I instantly think to myself about where the husband is. He has either run off with a younger, prettier version of the lady with no personality whatsoever, or he is away working and not considering the struggles that one will face on a flight with a toddler.

I then realise how cynical I am being judging these poor people who may have perfectly happy lives, and I return to my inner chaos. I do note that this brief period of being an overanalysing bitch did remove me from everything momentarily, so at least that is a positive snippet to my torture.

The aircraft begins to manoeuvre down the runway, and the airhostesses perform their usual safety briefing, which has become quite lazy I record, since my first experiences of flying. I remember watching them back then in awe at how much effort they put in, but now after pointing out the exits, they hand you a laminated card to figure most other aspects for yourself.

Safety is the last of my worries, I think, and quite frankly, it would make my life a lot easier if we did crash. A thought which I instantly retract because I would never be so selfish towards my loving children who are innocently unaware of the torment I am going through right now.

As we ascend into the air, I go over the past few months in my head and how dramatically my life has yet again been flipped on its head. Just two months prior to everything that has happened, I was feeling quite content with my life and excited for our trip to Dublin. Of course, I had nerves about meeting Brannagh in person for the first time, but I hadn't a clue as to how bad things were with her and how much of a nightmare our trip was going to turn out to be. Despite all that had already gone on over the past five years, I had come through stronger and probably happier than I ever was before, but now all that progress has been ripped away from me as if it was attached only by a Velcro fastener.

The refreshments trolley passes me, and I almost retch at the thought of consuming anything, the smell of coffee that always brings such pleasure is driving my insides insane. The lady notices this movement and avoids directing her offer of snacks to me entirely and swiftly moves on down the aisle. I shock myself as I can't even consume another drop of alcohol, especially as it isn't doing its usual job properly in calming my nerves. If it were an employee of mine, it would definitely get the sack after today's performance.

I get my headphones out of my bag and aimlessly stare out at the passing clouds while playing my favourite songs but not taking any lyrics in. In fact, if the man next to me asks me what I am listening to, I won't be able to tell him. Nothing is taking away the feeling of total dread for the next few days, so I decide simply to accept this and wish the time away to be with Eileen sooner.

Finally, we touch down on Irish soil, and I look up to the air-conditioning unit to desperately ask for the help and support from somebody above. I stretch as if I have just woken from a deep sleep, but actually it's to straighten myself up from all the torment that is going on inside of me. My phone is vibrating, and I look at the time to see that the flight is twenty minutes delayed. Eileen is obsessed with punctuality, so she will be worried, but I don't answer. I need a moment to compose myself before speaking to anybody that I know for fear that I will openly crumble.

As we are ushered off the plane and along the tarmac to the baggage reclaim area, I text Eileen to tell her that I am on my way, still avoiding talking to her. The conveyer belt hasn't started moving yet which gives me more time to strengthen up before being reunited with my aunt, but then I ask myself why I am worrying because if I break down to anybody over the next few days, Eileen is who will help the most.

I shut my eyes and pray inwardly while waiting for action to begin in the baggage reclaim, thanking God for making me pack too much stuff, so I had to put my luggage in the hold as well as asking for so much strength as I have asked for so many times before. I realise how lovely the feeling is to close my eyes and literally shut off from everything, but the images inside my head soon force me to reopen them.

My bag is one of the first to come around, so I am forced to head to arrivals where Eileen is waiting. My bottom lip begins to tremble as soon as I see her welcoming face with her arms held out, and I run up to her as if I am still a child wanting so desperately to jump into her arms but realising that I have gained a few pounds since those days. For the first few moments we don't say a word, but so much is being said through our long embrace, and we head to the car to prepare ourselves. I hadn't contemplated that Eileen may be feeling quite worried about meeting Sheila too.

'The table is booked for 7,' Eileen throws at me while we're putting my bags into the boot of her car, and everything suddenly becomes more real.

'Thank you,' I say, breaking once again inside.

'Sorry to put it like that, I just felt that a meal wouldn't be so intense. At least you can chop up your steak to reset yourself if things get too much.'

I laugh at Eileen's thought process but feel very grateful for how sensitive she is being about the whole situation, and we head to her house to mentally prepare ourselves.

After a short sleep, which Eileen suggested I had to shut off and regain some life, and a few more glasses of wine, I am feeling ready. I am feeling strong and want to leave right now so that this feeling doesn't leave me. However, we still have to wait another twenty minutes which I know is going to seem like the longest twenty minutes I have ever had.

I am happy with how I look today, which is one good thing about it all. Daddy gave me some money for a new dress for the occasion for this very reason, and I am happy with my purchase. Eileen is never one to comment on looks because

195

she's all about how people are inside but even *she* has directed a few compliments my way already this evening.

I watch the clock intently while sipping my last drops of my second glass, still not giving me that soothing feeling, and eventually it reaches twenty to seven, so I grab my bag and wait for Eileen to do all of the safety checks around her house before leaving that her paranoia forces her to do.

During the journey to the restaurant, I consider how different this trip to Dublin is from the start of our trip before. I think about how even though there was the underlying discomfort regarding my meeting with Brannagh, the time that I spent with the children beforehand was thoroughly enjoyable and even normal.

I remember how excited Jack had been about the zoo and how he chatted away to me in almost a comprehensible manner. I laugh at how even Erin removed her earplugs for a split second to take on board what the driver was saying, showing genuine interest. I smile at how lucky we were with the weather and how well it reflected my mood as it is doing now—raining, windy and cold.

We arrive at Skinflint on Dame Street, and Eileen looks as though she wants to hug me but instead grabs my hand and tells me that everything is going to be okay. Her warm hand in mine gives me the push I need to enter the restaurant. I silently thank her for this knowing that another hug would have destroyed my strength, and we head inside.

Luckily, Sheila is yet to arrive, and we are directed to our table in a nice, cosy corner lit up by candles enhancing the calm atmosphere. A calm atmosphere but not a very calm me, particularly when a blonde lady whose face isn't as familiar as I remember walks through the door and smiles nervously at myself and Eileen. Here we go; I think to myself, this is it.

Chapter 25
Dublin, 2018

The tall blonde heads our way after informing the welcoming waiter that we are the company that she is meeting. Sheila is taller than I remember and looks more sophisticated and stronger now than she did when I saw her at the police station a few months ago. She is wearing a tight, knee length navy blue dress and heels which I think is a bit fancy for the occasion but then remember about the effort I have put in, so I allow for this same effort on her part too.

As she comes towards the table, I get a whiff of her Dior fragrance, a smell that I am very fond of. Mammy always wore Dior, and for my twenty-fifth birthday one of the many thoughtful gifts from Daddy was this perfume. Though it wasn't the exact smell that Mammy wore, the aroma kept her with me, and even to this day I always have some on my dresser at home.

I follow Eileen's lead in greeting Sheila because she has that inner strength thing nailed, even when she is hurting inside. I, on the other hand, haven't mastered this skill and don't think I ever will, especially in situations such as this one. We decided back at the house that we will avoid the formal handshake and instead perform a friendly kiss on the cheek, maybe even a little hug given the circumstances of our meet.

She sits opposite us both, and I can feel the tension on the table. Her facial expression is emphatically false, and even though I don't know the lady well, I can tell she is struggling to keep her guard up. I can feel the tears that want to burst out of her eyes like a waterfall that never stops running. I can see the true heartbroken expression that she so desperately wants to portray but knows that she can't. I want to tell her that she can. My heart hurts for the poor lady. Instead, I decide to begin with some light-hearted conversation to break us in before getting down to the serious matters of tomorrow's arraignment in court.

'I love that perfume you're wearing. Dior, isn't it?' I say, feeling that a compliment is something that she needs right now.

'Yes. I absolutely love it, always have.'

'That's amazing.'

I pause a moment, wanting to say how Mammy used to wear Dior and how Daddy bought it for me on my twenty-fifth birthday. I want to tell her that it is something that I am always in possession of and that when I wear it or when I smell its fragrance that Mammy is instantly back here with me. However, I refrain, and I am thankful that I do because it would be highly inappropriate to mention Mammy today of all days. One day perhaps we will get to that point, but today and the next few months it is all about Brannagh.

I then realise that the words *that's amazing* may appear an odd response without explanation because most women always wear a particular scent. It's normal; there is nothing amazing about it. To be frank, *amazing* was an entirely wrong choice of vocabulary in this instance. I think to myself, *just leave it, Mary, you've enough to worry about you don't need to stress about how the conversation should have gone.*

'Right, let's order some wine and starters, shall we?' Eileen says, breaking the silence with a positive suggestion.

'Oh yes, I need it,' Sheila replies, creating a perfect platform for me to bring up the elephant in the room.

'Sheila, you know. We are so sorry,' I say, prompting the beginning of the conversation we should have started twenty minutes ago but also expressing my genuine sympathies.

'Thank you,' comes her reply, not allowing room for more on the topic. I ignore her closing comment and say my piece.

'I don't want to make this dinner solemn, but I want to tell you now that myself and Eileen are completely on your side. I may not have known Brannagh in person for long, but we shared years of friendship through the letters we wrote, so we sort of built a strong connection that way.'

'Letters?' Sheila's reply stumps me, as it is so unexpected.

'I thought you were so close, I thought she'd have told you. We wrote to each other all the time. From when I moved to England right up until a few months back when we finally met in person. She was the person that I turned to whenever I was having issues, and I think I may have been the same to her too.'

'That's lovely. She never said.'

I am happy that I have chosen to bring up the topic of our letter writing as it has opened many avenues for the conversation to go down a positive route. I knew this meet would have sadness all over it, but if we could talk about good memories of Brannagh, I could tell Sheila all about the letters, and maybe she could inform me of more about who my half-sister really was.

'Yes, it was nice. We kept up to date almost weekly through our letters. Of course, at times our lives were too busy to continue, like when I started college and when she went off to boarding school. You know, new things in our lives meant that we couldn't write so much, but we still managed to stay in touch most of the time.'

I wanted to express my confusion over the fact that Brannagh was only five years younger than me, yet Sheila and Daddy told everyone so convincingly that their affair had only been going on for three years. No more than three years, they told me. I could feel the frustration returning from years ago and anger filling me, knowing how big a lie that was. The maths simply doesn't add up. I let it go and tune back into our conversation.

'I bet she told you what an awful mother I was shipping her off to boarding school, didn't she?'

'No. Quite the opposite actually. She always said good things about you, and she wrote about the fondest memories which were mostly with you too.'

'That's so good to hear.'

We both pause the conversation to take a sip of our wine, and I realise that this is a useful discussion to have for both of us. Sheila clearly has paranoia as to what Brannagh truly thought of her as a mother, and there is so much that I never got to learn about Brannagh due to the gaps that letter writing left, so through our chat we can both be satisfied by what is being spoken about.

I look over to Eileen who smiles at me, with that smile that tells me telepathically that I am doing great. She knows how nervous I am and how hard I am trying not to let the past taint my treatment of Sheila, so her look of approval helps me to go on.

'In fact, I think she loved boarding school after she had got used to it and settled in.

She certainly made some great friends there. I think Si– '

'Simon,' Sheila interrupts.

'Yes, they were very good friends, weren't they? She spoke about him a lot.'

'Ah, this is great to hear. I always had this awful image of her crying in her room each night. Now I know that she was probably writing to you. I only sent her there because it was such a prestigious school, and I felt it would do her the world of good to get away from Dublin and meet new friends. She was never very sociable at school and lacked confidence hugely, but when she returned home her confidence blossomed.'

'See, that's something that I never got to see. You can't suss out how confident someone is from a letter. They could get behind a pen and come across as the most self-assured person, but they could be so shy in reality. It saddens me. And I know we can never bring her back, but over time I can still get to know her a bit better through your thoughts and memories, a positive take on a god-awful situation.'

'I like your thinking. Thank you. She was the best thing.'

Apart from the minor blip in the middle, my thoughts have been solely with Brannagh throughout this conversation. I admit that my focus has occasionally slipped to how delicious the wine we are drinking is and how easily it is sliding down my throat, but mostly I've been with Brannagh. We have already finished bottle number one which is the second bottle for Eileen and I having consumed one before we left, so it's almost time to order another when my mind starts up again into panic mode.

Tomorrow we are all attending the court hearing where Daniel will be formally charged, and the terrible crime that he committed will be read out to all who can hear once more. We were told that there was no need to attend and that not everyone does attend the arraignment, however, we all wanted to be involved in every moment so that we could witness him getting the punishment he deserves which would never be satisfactory compared to what he has done to our lives.

It took the police force no time at all to find evidence of him being at the scene of the crime when they discovered his DNA plastered all over the kitchen and living room, yet he still denied it all. This sickens me, thinking how he could be so inhuman and when the victim was such a beautiful girl as Brannagh, a girl that he never deserved.

Of course, he has a platform to deny all charges because after all he was known to go to Sheila's house fairly frequently, being the boyfriend of her daughter, but Sheila claims he hadn't been around in a few months after everything had worsened between them, yet the evidence discovered by police was fresh.

Despite, never meeting Daniel before Brannagh's death and only hearing about his cruel ways from Brannagh herself, who I am still convinced was sugar-coating matters somewhat, since this court case my bad opinions have strengthened no end. Especially, after he denied any abuse within their relationship and claimed it was very healthy, and that they were getting along fine. I saw the bruises and the scars. I witnessed her tears. Therefore, as biased as the opinion I hold may be, I fully believe every word that Brannagh told me.

I am suddenly brought back into the moment when the waiter asks whether or not we are ready to order, and I realise that my mind has been elsewhere while Eileen, and Sheila have been choosing their starters and mains.

'You two go first, I can't decide,' I say to mask my momentary absence.

'I'll have the Viv pizza please,' Eileen says with confidence, probably having known what she was going to order from the moment she woke up this morning. I know what she is like.

'And I will have the Dorothy,' Sheila says afterwards, and at that moment, I notice my concentration hasn't yet returned because I am clueless as to why they are saying female names rather than pizza toppings.

I glance down at the menu, realise the way that it is set out and choose to go for the Nora, chuckling slightly at my order but happily feeling part of the gang again. Bloody Nora. We share a garlic bread for starters which thankfully is simply placed on the menu with its correct title rather than a female forename.

I am now officially back in the room and hope to God that my company was too distracted with their orders to notice my previous distance. I pour more wine into each of our glasses which empties the remainder of the first bottle, and I signal the waiter for more. He smiles and nods at me, probably being far too judgemental, but right now I frankly couldn't care.

With every new glass prior to this one, we have had a cheers because we need all the luck and good fortune that we can get our hands on. Besides, we're Irish, so you can never say cheers to enough things in life. So, to continue our meal tradition so far, I decide to make this the glass in honour of giving us the strength we need for tomorrow.

'To us getting the outcome that we need tomorrow,' I say, keeping my fingers crossed and wincing a little, hoping that my suggestion goes down well.

Granted I am feeling a little tipsy, so I have built the confidence to say more than I would have at the beginning of our dinner, however, these are things that need to be addressed, so I am glad to be the one that is doing so.

'Cheers!' comes my thankful response, and I am both relieved and happy that I dedicated this glass to the event.

'You know, it's going to be seriously difficult to see his face again. I always thought him a lovely lad, but now, obviously, my opinions have changed entirely, and I just want to rip him apart. I never thought I could kill, but now I know that I could.'

It is after Sheila has finished her miniature rant that I realise she too is probably feeling a little drunk, and that is why the truth is all coming out. Being so reserved at first, I thought this dinner was going to exhaust me, but now the conversation, and the correct conversation at that, is coming so smoothly.

'Did you know anything about the way he treated Brannagh?' I ask her, genuinely shocked at Brannagh not asking her mother for help but rather coming to a total stranger in a different country—me.

'Nothing,' she pauses, and something appears to be on her mind. 'I suppose occasionally she seemed a little distressed after seeing him, or she would shut me off and just retreat to her room, but I always assumed that was down to her being on her period or that they had had an argument. It was never clear that something was *actually* wrong.'

'That's so sad that she couldn't speak to any of us. I mean, she tried to tell me, and I guess it's easier telling an almost stranger than your mother, but even then I am convinced she wasn't telling me truly how bad it was.'

The service in the restaurant is great, and I glance at my watch to check the time once we finish our mains. I can't believe it is only half past nine, it feels as though we have been here much longer than that. I suppose the intensity of the conversation has prolonged time, but still, I would have expected it to be at least an hour later than it is. However, we're all tired, and with a big day tomorrow we decide to take ourselves off to our separate beds, despite Eileen offering Sheila a glass back at her house.

I am glad Sheila declined this offer because I am tired but also wanted to debrief with my aunt on my own before tomorrow. We both feel that our meeting with Sheila went as well as it could have gone and that we covered many bases of difficult conversational topics. As a reward to us both for getting through it and to temporarily lessen our dread for tomorrow, we open a bottle of Champagne, a staple ingredient to the contents of Eileen's fridge.

Chapter 26
Dublin, 2018

I can't remember whether we finished the bottle of Champagne, but judging by my headache that I have woken with this morning, I feel as though we did. I go into the kitchen to make Eileen and me a cup of tea before getting ready for the hard day ahead. We sit in silence partly because of our dreadful hangovers but partly due to fear about the outcome of today. I have my outfit laid out, so getting ready shouldn't be too difficult, but as I sit with Eileen and our cups of tea, I want to pause life and remain in that moment forever.

My mobile starts to ring, and it is Dad and the kids, so I have to answer as much as right now I don't want to. Trying to pretend that all is okay is the hardest thing especially when hearing their familiar voices makes me want to weep. I remain strong as they send their love and Erin tells me all that she has been up to at school. She speaks on behalf of Jack which tells me that there has been no miraculous change there, and Daddy sounds exhausted, but hopefully, I think to myself, all will be resolved today. Well, mostly. For it to be resolved we would have Brannagh back, but that can never happen, sadly.

I hang up and get up to get dressed when Eileen comes through already ready and stops me in her tracks with an affectionate gesture.

'It's going to be okay, darling.'

With her comforting statement I begin to cry, and she hugs me so tightly giving me the strength to go on.

'We are all going to be strong. For Brannagh.'

Sternness fills the building when we enter the courtroom, and I am reminded of being back at school in Dublin in an assembly with our strict head teacher. He was fine once you got on his side, but from first impressions, he was terrifying. We sit nervously, and the procedure begins.

'All rise. Judge Melinda presiding. Please be seated.'

The judge's voice beckons through the eerie room which is well heated yet still feels cold, and I blame that on the circumstances. I scout around the room to see who I recognise, trying to avoid making eye contact with him. It's like a funeral when the family are seated at the front. You never look back to see who's there, you don't much care, and it isn't the thing to do. This feels the same, but I so desperately want to know.

I think of how I can glance but make it look as though I am not doing so. As if I am exercising my neck due to pain or having a stretch but taking in the faces within the room while I do. In a panic about how obvious I am being, I look too far to the right and cannot believe my eyes. Daniel is absent and too much a familiar face is standing in his place. A face that haunts me and puts a sheet of darkness over many of my childhood memories. A face I'd have liked to forget completely, but he will never let that happen.

Chapter 27
York, 2016

Mary knew that her mother would be turning in her grave if she was aware about all her inner thoughts and plans that had gone around her head over the past few months. She was thankful that her father wasn't as strictly catholic as Anna was and that he had moved his views into modern times with regards to things like contraception and the dreaded D word. He still went to Mass, often lit a candle and would always thank God on good days so his faith remained; it had just become less prominent in his later years.

Mary had tried so hard to stay strong since James' injury, but every day she found it more difficult. The children were doing great, though they had their fair share of wobbles, and Mary was the only one available to pick up the pieces of their broken family and try to force it back together. Each time the process became more difficult, and she felt as though she had chosen another wrong piece of the jigsaw, and each time that piece was further from the right fit.

The hospital visits were tiresome, and James' recovery hadn't gone to plan which made her efforts seem worthless. She wanted to keep up her endeavour, but each day when she got into the car, she found herself dragging more parts of her body that were reluctant to join.

Often, she felt like she was two separate people inside one frame. One version of herself was determined to continue, to remain strong and to appear to have it all together. She wanted her children to look up to her and think how amazingly strong she was. She wanted to continue with the visits and continue to love her husband of seventeen years. She tried to keep faith and cling onto the idea that he would come home and recover from all of this and that their lives were going to go back to normal as if this treacherous three-year episode of hell had never happened. She always was a dreamer.

The other version was about ready to crumble into a pile of tiny little pieces of emptiness on the floor. A heap of failure. Not wanting to continue with the hospital visits. Not wanting to stay strong for anyone. Not wanting to love her husband who had changed so drastically and so fast into nothing like the man she fell for. Not having faith in anything.

The original twelve-month recovery period as predicted by the specialist during the first month after James was admitted soon changed with further bleeds on his brain, operations to fix these problems only for the brain to bleed some more. Mary had a selection of medical language bouncing around her head along with the whirlwind of negative thoughts. Words like hydrocephalus, sepsis and posttraumatic amnesia. They were all things that James had suffered but words that she wished she had never needed to learn the meaning of.

She hated herself for having such thoughts, but Mary would frequently sit by James' bedside, wishing he had died. She thought about how much easier it would have been if the incident had killed him rather than it being as it was and James being that one percent that survived. She then questioned whether he had really survived and whether the state he was currently in could be classed as a full survival. He had no quality of life, and he wasn't the James she knew any longer, so who was he?

She knew that *easier* wasn't the correct word to use, as no outcome was easy. Yet if death was the outcome then as devastated as herself and the children would have been, they could have mourned the loss of James and moved on. They could have gone through the process of grieving as so many people do every day and continued their lives, though with a broken heart, with good memories too rather than the imprint that this process was grinding into her memory. It was so damaging to all of them.

She hated herself for these thoughts, but they couldn't be helped, and she figured it was only a natural human reaction to such a situation. Dealing with death was easier than dealing with the heartache of watching someone you once so passionately loved change, suffer and potentially die anyway.

Mary was told a different version of events almost daily, and she initially got infuriated by this desperately seeking the truth, for someone to tell her that everything was going to be all right and for that someone to genuinely mean it. However, after time she realised that even the specialists found James' condition rare and complex, so they weren't playing her or failing at their job but rather they hadn't got a clue because they hadn't come across these circumstances before. It was a huge learning experience for everyone involved, and as agonising as Mary found it, she had to understand this.

Mary had only told her dad when she went to the solicitors to get the correct papers for the divorce, and she had only told one person because of the guilt she felt within her. It was a decision that she had toyed with for months, but things had got too much for her to handle, and she couldn't move on from it all or even have a break while she still remained committed to James. Not only that, but financial advisers and people in the legal field of work suggested that a divorce may benefit them both in the future from the point of view of the law.

She admitted to her dad after she told him that it was a crazy move and she probably wasn't in the most stable mindset to make such a choice, however, she couldn't see another route out of the mess. She promised she would remain loyal in the sense that she still cared for James hugely and would continue with the hospital visits, but she had to get out of the entrapment that she felt through their being entwined, mixed up even, inside a marriage.

The final straw was during another of James' violent episodes, a stage that James' behaviour had been through a few times and seemed to keep going around in a loop, repeating each stage near enough identically. It was as if each stage was a track on the playlist that was James' recovery, so it was never going to change, and some tracks Mary preferred massively compared to others. His violence occurred usually every third stage, so at least she had a bit of a break in between she always thought, gripping tightly onto the positive aspects of all of this wherever she could.

The first time she witnessed the behaviour changing dramatically was, of course, the hardest. After he had threatened members of staff and grabbed Mary herself quite forcefully enough times for experts to view him as a danger to himself and others, he was moved to a specialist unit for brain injuries just outside of Leeds. A brain rehabilitation hospital. Not only did this make Mary's life logistically more difficult having to travel further to visit James, so reducing the visits to once or twice a week as opposed to daily, it made her mental struggle even more unbearable.

She couldn't be sure that the children would be okay visiting having only just eased them into the visits at the hospital. It was all too distressing for them. She never knew what state he would be in at the new unit and whether he would lash out at one of the children, never meaning to but not being in control of his actions. She tried to avoid taking them at all, but they still wanted to see their dad, and none of them knew how long he would be around to visit, so equally she didn't want to deny anybody of this time with him.

As for Mary, she hated going to see him for the first few months at the rehabilitation trust because she was quite frankly terrified. She knew it was her wifely duty to continue the visits, and she did still love the man who James used to be, but the version after the incident was horrible, and she hoped and prayed every night that it was only temporary.

For the first few months during the first violent episode, Mary would travel an hour down the road, trembling with nerves, arrive and usually have to call security within five minutes of seeing James because he would have gone to hit her or held her up against a wall by the neck. She always thought about Sarah in the film *Love Actually* visiting her brother, and how sorry she had always felt for her, but now how much she could relate.

James had developed a strong vengeance towards Mary, not understanding the reasoning behind his being in there. He naturally blamed her for everything and had got it into his head that she put him there in some controlling and manipulative act of cruelty. He hadn't told her he loved her in months. He hadn't shown her any affection in years. They hadn't had a proper conversation since it all happened, and he never asked about the children. She often wondered if he knew that they existed.

Mary always thanked God that the drive home from the unit was just over an hour long because it allowed her time to grieve. To grieve the man she hadn't yet lost but felt she lost years ago. To grieve their solid relationship and her having a partner by her side to discuss life's many problems with, and to celebrate their wonderful family. To grieve her best friend.

The most recent incident took Mary over the edge, and she asked to see a specialist immediately hoping that they could give her answers. As she sat down in Dr Clooney's room, she broke down in tears, no longer able to hold it together for everybody. Dr Clooney expressed his sympathies with as much understanding as he could for somebody who didn't understand at all, and Mary thanked him genuinely for his efforts.

'Mrs Carter, I realise this is extremely difficult for you, and it is also something that we can't be black and white about. Our thoughts at the beginning were, indeed, that James would make a full recovery, not without side effects, but as close to a recovery as was possible within a twelve-month period. Now obviously, with complications, especially the two serious further bleeds on the brain, things are much more complex, and I can't be sure that the case remains the same as it did at the start. I'm very sorry.'

Mary said nothing. The pause urged Dr Clooney to continue.

'There are organisations out there to help you, you know. And we will obviously give you all the support that we can during such a difficult time.'

Mary hated the expression *such a difficult time* because it was one that was used so flippantly at any given change of circumstances no matter where it lay on the level of bad. When her mother died, it was a difficult time as were her frequent arguments with James during their first year together, but both were very different levels of difficult. Another expression she was getting sick of which was frequently uttered by medical staff was *everybody's different.* Hearing those words changed nothing and gave her not one ounce of relief.

Mary adjusted her seated position in the chair of the consultant's office to remind herself that this was all real because it was very easy to hide away and pretend that she was living in a fantasy world, a world she wished was false. She knew that it wasn't Dr Clooney's job to counsel her on whether a divorce was a horrible, immoral move, but she so desperately wanted to pour out her thoughts and feelings about why she was wavering towards that decision.

She wanted Clooney to act for a brief moment in the place that James used to fill but no longer was a part of, and she wanted to tell him all her woes no matter how small or ridiculous. It helped that he was fairly easy on the eye, so his looks would compare with how James used to be. However, it wasn't his job, so she left it and the room, taking only her ever-weakening body and soul to the car park.

She had hoped that the appointment with the consultant would have answered the mass of questions inside her, and that her visit directly after the appointment to the solicitors regarding their divorce would be made easier because of this. However, it only created space for a further questioning of her actions, and for the first time since she had firmly decided upon the break up route, Mary felt evil.

Mary wept as she left the solicitors having been convinced that for now a separation was the most plausible option after she had spent hours filling in the correct documents. She felt as though she had left half of her existence behind but a part that she couldn't get back. She no longer had faith that things would ever be as they were before, and she had no idea how she was going to break the news to the children.

Tears continued to fall as she entered the family home and fell into her father's arms. Her father who had held her through everything in her life and continued to do so. She lay sinking deeper and deeper into his warm body like a little girl. She had officially crumbled worse than ever before. A bottle of red wine stood opened on the coffee table from the night before when she thought to herself that for the time being drinking was no answer at all.

Chapter 28
17 December 2017

As the car pulled up to the crematorium, the huge crowd of people overwhelmed me as I sat in between my two littlest rocks, Erin and Jack, both weeping uncontrollably. We had requested that the coffin went in before we did mostly for the sake of the children and then we were to enter followed by the rest of the mourners, whose ages highlighted James' short life.

It was incredible how the outcome that I had previously prayed for had now happened, but I found it so much harder than I thought I would. I thought it would bring closure and relief when I heard the inevitable news having remained loyal until his death, but instead it broke me once more. The thousands of tiny pieces that made me split in halves and quarters, requiring even more strength to build me back up. Strength that I simply didn't have anymore.

James' parents couldn't have been more supportive through my decision last year, but I still hurt inside whenever I saw them, especially now with emptiness filling their faces. Sally was dressed in a knee length black dress with thick tights and a black hat. It was something that they had joked about during the hospital visits that she would wear her best hat to his funeral because she hated the hat, so wished that it would never happen. Attending their own child's funeral was something that no parent should have to go through. It was the most unnatural thing in the world, and something I learned early on witnessing Grandma O'Sullivan weeping by Mammy's gravestone.

As we approached the entrance to the crematorium, I squeezed both children into me as tightly as I could. I wanted to show them I cared. I wanted to apologise to them for not being as strong as they wanted me to be. I wanted to say sorry for separating from their father. Most of all, I wanted them to stay strong for me. How selfish we humans can be.

We made our way out of the car directed by the undertakers, and I wished I hadn't worn heels because I was too unsteady on my legs to walk properly in them. I wished the pews to be closer than they were, or to park up at the back and remain discreet, lessening the chance of me falling over, showing how I was feeling both physically and metaphorically.

Katie Melua's cover of *What a Wonderful World* came out strongly from the speakers because James always saw the goodness in everything and everyone. I was overtaken by past memories that left out the horror of the final years. I was remembering the happy times when our family was one and the times before we had a family at all when we loved every aspect that life threw our way. I could hear Sally crying next to Jack who didn't know how to react in the situation he was in. His first funeral, and it was for his dad. Life can be so cruel.

Readings came from the reverend who reeled off all of our blurbs put together mixed in with religious connotations of what he felt that death was to him. *Abide with Me* was the chosen hymn, but my voice box failed me due to my weakness and my tears, so I enjoyed the sound of the organ playing a favourite of mine. The committal was spoken, and the curtains closed, giving us all closure to a long-suffering horrendous incident. The brain is such a powerful organ. At least, our James suffers no more.

As we exited the building for the part of a funeral that any family member dreads, I took Erin and Jack by the hands to the bouquet that some minutes before lay rested where their father was.

'Take a daisy each,' I urged to them, both looking fearful at ruining a beautiful display of flowers, 'go on, you're allowed to.' They each took their favourite coloured bud and cautiously held it in their small hands. 'Now whenever you're missing Daddy, press on this for comfort. He is always going to be with you.' Erin smiled, and Jack remained looking confused as we edged our way to stand and be sent many condolences from everybody who loved James.

A true character. A lovely soul. Kind and thoughtful, always giving his everything. Wonderful. Brilliant. Charming. These were all their words; he was all mine.

Chapter 29
28 August 2018

I feel sick and desperately want to vacate the room in order to vomit. To vomit everywhere. To vomit up everything life has thrown at me, and to start again. I am taken back to school days in the examination hall when I used to turn to the first question on the exam paper and feel sick at my cluelessness, wishing I had revised more for the test.

My hands are trembling, as are my legs and my feet. In fact, my whole body has turned weak, weaker now than I have been throughout the entire turmoil of events. I can't believe it. Daddy never mentioned when we were staying with him all those years ago, but he did always say that one of my uncles on Mammy's side was slightly dodgy and always hiding something. Yet he was such a good support during everything that went on in those days, so I guess we all just masked his wicked ways.

In my head wreck I realise that the room has gone blurry and I have muted the sound of the speaker entirely, tuning back in to hear the address of the horrid crime. I immediately tune back out. I don't think I can listen to it now, not again, not under this turn of events.

I knew it was going to be hard to witness Daniel standing there, probably looking cocky and smug, and creating a wave of anger within me almost turning me red with it all. However, this is worse. So much worse, and anger isn't the emotion that I most feel but rather sickness and vulgar for the truth to be so far from what I thought to be true.

I look down at my smart trousers appreciating Eileen's wardrobe choice in making me feel like I look good when I feel so horrible inside. I have always had that ability to look good in trousers and not like a man. I can pull off the lady trouser suit combination and still look feminine. I put this down to my figure and dainty facial features, like those girls who suit very short haircuts; I am one of those. I have never been brave enough to cut my hair off though I know it will suit me. It is one of the few things I feel good about sometimes and Erin has luckily inherited these features from me as I always planned for my daughter. I would have hated for Jack to have got the feminine dainty looks and Erin have been given broad shoulders like James had. I know it happens to some unfortunate families but not in mine.

These thoughts aren't going to change anything no matter how good they make me briefly feel. I think back to the time that I spent with him when I was just a little girl. All those hours in the garden dead heading his plants and picking fruit to use in my baking with his wife. Was she his wife? So many hours when we were alone together. I wonder what he was thinking inside his cruel mind.

I realise that my emotions are lessening to the feeling of emptiness inside me, and I feel crazy for this so tune back in to hear what the judge is saying, none of which I wish to listen to again, but I know that I have to face it. I glance at Eileen whose smile once again strengthens me and I listen, for the first time during this hearing, intently.

'For the murder of Brannagh McDinton.'

I quickly absence myself unable yet to face hearing the name of the accused out loud. But Brannagh was so convincing in all she said about Daniel, I think quietly to myself, he is still an awful person. But perhaps he isn't. Perhaps I need to meet him to find out for myself. Was all that she said about him actually about someone else? Maybe Daniel's name was a substitute for the real brute.

It suddenly dawns on me that through the whole episode of the trial for the murder of my beloved sister, I have been so convinced that Daniel was the culprit that I missed the huge details. I never asked questions I merely assumed.

When I heard that they had discovered a significant amount of evidence in fingerprints at the scene, I assumed it was the slimy prints of Daniel's guilty hands. When I heard that they had made an arrest and a confident arrest at that, I assumed they had handcuffed Daniel. When I heard that he pleaded not guilty on the first accusation, my anger was directed towards Daniel. When I received the date of the hearing, that in which we are currently sat, I thought so strongly that I would witness the face of Daniel stood before the court, still trying to get away with what he had done. Never assume.

I resort to practising my mindfulness exercises that Dr Knoll once taught me when I was struggling with another soap opera worthy event that my life decided to put upon me. My feelings were just like they are now, and my mind wouldn't focus on anything, particularly not the issues I needed to resolve.

The hour-drive home from the unit in which James resided became less therapeutic and more like torture. I didn't feel safe to drive, so Dr Knoll suggested meditation for five minutes beforehand on a new application on my iPhone. I was only getting to grips with answering calls and sending texts let alone extracurricular activities on the device, but I took her simple instructions, and it helped. Erin would have been so proud.

I was then told how to be in the moment by focussing on my breathing and only that. This was harder than it sounds, but the effects were incredible. I would be like *Winnie the Pooh* in A. A. Milne's fantastic collection. Spotting objects out of the window like my children still do when we are going on long journeys to try to make the journey go faster.

That's it, I was very much like a child, simplifying everything and being totally in the moment. Tree. House. Sky. Bird. Train. Bridge. Cow. Road.

I try to practise this method now in the courtroom, though the scenes aren't quite as happy as those in the Yorkshire countryside. Desk. Judge. Tall ceiling. Lawyers. Sad faces. Darkness.

I quickly realise that my descriptions are becoming too gloomy to give me the benefits that the exercise usually performs, and I turn to stage one of my mindfulness programme that Dr Knoll thought was so valuable to someone like me. Back to basics.

I breathe in for two seconds and out all the way until my lungs feel empty. I breathe in for three seconds and out again. I can feel people's eyes glancing at me, but I don't care. I am allowed to be a little crazy. Besides, I always have been, so why change that now when I absolutely can be.

I breathe in for four seconds and out again. Each time breathing in through my nose and out through my mouth, just like it says on my application. Then in for five and out. I want to start all over again.

Five is usually where you go back to one because most people struggle with a five-second in breath let alone any more. Sometimes when you reach five seconds, you feel okay enough to continue living. Sometimes you need to repeat the process once more completely or at least redo half of it and then you can continue with your day. Whatever you need.

Today five isn't enough, but I am not in private nor do I have access to private, so I must continue living before feeling comfortable enough to do so. It's okay if you're out in public on a bus or shopping and nobody will notice your breathing, but inside a quiet, formal courtroom everybody notices everything. I must be strong. The glances stop and return to the focus of the room as my thoughts stop my exaggerated breathing. I am sure everybody was just concerned.

I return to the focus and have lost track entirely of who is who within the courtroom. This is the first trial that I have been to, and with it being so personal to me, I would have expected to be a little delirious at times, but I have watched so many crime dramas on the television that I feel I should at least know everybody's role within the room. Currently, the only person I can put a job title to is the judge which isn't exactly rocket science considering the uniform.

'What's your name?' comes in a demanding tone from a man dressed smartly in a navy-blue suit. I gather he must be a lawyer.

I still feel reluctant to face the reality and wish to tune out for the reply, but my powers seem to have left me. That is one of my favourite skills in life and a skill that I have developed through the trials and tribulations that life has sweetly provided for me. I have always, in times of need, been capable of mentally rather than physically leaving the room. That way I don't make it obvious, but I give my brain and body a minute to recuperate. I call it my superpower, and if I were a superhero then it is the skill I would possess. This time (for the first time, however), my powers have failed me, and I must face acknowledging the painful truth.

'Derek O'Sullivan,' my sheepishly weak Uncle replies, his head turning slightly towards the ground in shame but still trying to maintain the correct etiquette for court. Positioned as if he were at a barbershop.

'You are charged with the murder of Brannagh McDinton,' states the navy suit man, myself still failing to put a job role to his position.

Hearing my mother's maiden name on the other side of the trial seems wrong. Hearing my mother's maiden name brings a whole wave of emotions over me. There is so much that is wrong with this case. Questions begin to flood my mind as they have a habit of doing, all arriving at the same time like London buses. Derek, the friend who so kindly took us in and welcomed us to England wasn't a friend at all. My Uncle, another uncle to add to the list and an evil one at that. I don't want to be related to this monster, I thought he was such a nice man when we first arrived in England.

I wonder if Sheila is aware that Daniel might not be the culprit. Or maybe she has a vengeance towards Derek due to how helpful and supportive he was to my family through everything and not hers. Supposedly. As angry as I can be towards our shared past and where our lives uncomfortably crossed paths, having dined with her last night, I doubt she is the kind of person who would let a petty hatred end up in the courtroom like this one. That's the plot line for characters who end up on the *Jeremy Kyle show* or television programmes alike. She can't have known. This has to be the truth.

I look to analyse her face and decipher how much she knows about this incident that we do not. Her face saddens me to look at. It is pale and broken. Her eyes black not with running make up but rather bruising from so many tears, I think. Lack of sleep causes bruise coloured bags underneath your eyes, but Sheila's go that extra mile and look as though she has been punched. Punched with the heartbreak of losing her only child.

I feel absent from the room but still in it. Like those dreams that I often have which are of scenarios happening, usually with me a part in it but another me is watching. I am here but I am not. I don't think I will remember much of the proceedings anyway.

'Do you, Derek O'Sullivan, plead guilty or not guilty for the murder of Brannagh McDinton?' The judge puts so simply.

'Guilty.'

Bastard. I think.

Chapter 30
Dublin, 2018

'Darling, are you awake?' Eileen comes into the room in which I have been sleeping for I don't know how long. She always asks the most logical questions.

'Just about. Was I asleep for ages?'

'Only two days,' she says with a laugh.

It must be all over. That or it was all a dream, a nightmare, and I still have it upcoming in my events. I go to grab my phone to look at the date, maybe some text messages will help me figure out what I have been doing over the past few days, weeks, months. It all appears to have vanished from my memory like I so accurately predicted it would.

Eileen is shuffling some papers in the living room when she comes in with a letter from Daddy. Why he is writing me a letter I haven't a clue, but I gather we've not been in contact for the past few days because my last call to him is dated three days prior to the date of today. Maybe I really have been asleep all this time.

'Your daddy found out a lot sooner than you, but he didn't want to bring it up. Your life was going so well, and he wanted to keep all of this hidden away, never thinking it would come out. Especially, you being in England and all.'

Eileen's words are confusing me entirely as is the fact that she thinks I know what she is talking about. I feel, I should know, but I cannot remember past dinner with Sheila on Tuesday, and I am trying to think how to effectively explain this to Eileen without breaking her heart. I don't know how I should be feeling, but I feel nothing. I don't feel tired for the first time in months, potentially years, but I feel nothing else.

I guess the only way forward is to read the letter like a detective and figure where to go from there.

To my darling girl,
I hope to God that this letter never finds you because I strongly feel your life will be better without you having to face your past once again, but if it does, then I guess something pretty bad must have happened.

I know immediately that the letter isn't a recent one and that Daddy wrote it a while ago, good detective work. I continue.

I found out some crazy news today to add to the horrors of our past. More horrific for you. I don't know how else to put it but get straight to the point so that's what I'll do.
I am forever sorry for the hurt I caused you and your mother by being so selfish with my ways. Though I am not a wicked-hearted man and Sheila did mean something to me, I wholeheartedly loved and still love you and your mother unconditionally. I always will.

Daddy was not getting to the point like he said. He can never just get straight to the point.

'Sheila and I had an affair for seven years. We didn't plan things to happen how they did, but you will understand when you're older how life can just happen sometimes without you having any control at all.

When did Daddy write this? I must have been so young still. It must be important if he's kept it.

It started as a fling, and it got really out of hand, but what we certainly didn't expect was Brannagh to come out of it. However, I am no bastard, so I love Brannagh too unconditionally. After all, she is my child and I will love her forever, it is hopefully something that will be easier for you to understand as your grow. I am sorry.

Today, however, another factor was thrown into this mess churning it all up along with the feelings inside me. You sat at dinner tonight, and I wanted to talk to you. I wanted your mother to be here with us so badly. I wanted for us to be a family of three again.

Turns out your wicked Uncle Derek, who I have always thought a wrong one, he is the biological father of Brannagh. The man we are staying with. He who acted so genuine towards me offering to put a roof over our heads to make up for the guilt he felt. He, simultaneously, was having an affair with Sheila. An affair that I feel sick about. I hope you never have to find out, but sometimes, honesty is the best way.

I love you always, and I will still love Brannagh too,

Your Daddy. Xx

I turn the paper face down and place it onto the table, my jaw still wide open in shock. Eileen is hovering awkwardly in the doorway, ready to offer me a cup of tea or a hug, but currently, I can't think about the future, not even the next five minutes. Piecing everything together now has been instantly made so much easier. Every word Brannagh uttered about her horror story relationship was, in fact, the abuse she was receiving from her own father. That is why he moved to England. She had to keep so quiet for so many years. She reached out to me. I'm not sure which is worse. I feel sick.

Eileen senses my confusion and brings me a cup of tea and a digestive biscuit without asking. She sits beside me gently bringing her arm around me to give me a hug, probably scared that I will lash out because I am in so much shock. I don't think my head can take any more of this.

I want to say thank you, to thank her for being with me at every dramatic point in my life as well as the good parts too. I want to thank her for standing in as my mother, for giving me the time that my parents couldn't always give during my childhood. I want to thank her for my tea, my biscuit, and my hug. I can't speak. Words are jumbled bouncing around my head. They are the words that I so desperately want to grasp and put into long sentences of thanks, and maybe even an attempt at comprehending the pieces of my life. Fitting the new unexpected pieces in, and working out who I am. Who my family are.

Eventually, I find the courage to utter a sentence.

'I want to go home,' I say.

Home to my children. Home to my haven. Away from everything.